Meeting the Billionaire Boss

A billionaire marriage of convenience romance

In The Name of Love
Book 1

Wynter Wilde

For my family, friends and wonderful readers

Copyright © 2023 by WYNTER WILDE
All rights reserved.
No part of this book may be reproduced in any form or by any electronic or mechanical means, including information storage and retrieval systems, without written permission from the author, except for the use of brief quotations in a book review.

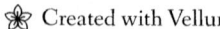 Created with Vellum

Meeting the Billionaire Boss – In the Name of Love Book 1

Edward Cavendish: Losing my wife two years ago was not something anyone expected. Lucille was beautiful and successful, and I thought we'd spend our lives together. Turns out I was wrong. Facing the world feels impossible so I shut myself away in my mansion in the countryside where only my young son can bring a smile to my face.

Ava Thorne: I'm broke. More than broke, actually. I have mountains of debt and it's getting worse by the day. I've been working two jobs to support my sick mother and younger brother, but when I'm fired from the one over a mistake that wasn't mine, I don't know where to turn.

Edward: My son's nanny is going away on the trip of a lifetime, so I need to find a replacement. It has to be someone we can trust but the thought of having anyone else in my home turns me cold. Plus, there's the inheritance clause that states I must be married on my 35th birthday and the date looms ever closer…

Ava: When the opportunity of a lifetime arises in the chance to earn a large sum of money fast, I'm forced to confront my past and decide if I can embrace a future I never dreamt of.

And it all starts with meeting the billionaire boss...

Chapter 1

Ava

'I'm sorry... I'm a bit confused.' I stare at the paperwork in my hand. 'Why exactly do I need to sign an NDA?'

Nala Fairweather shifts in her seat, runs a hand over her black braids, adjusts her navy silk blouse then places both hands flat on the desk in front of her. 'This is a brilliant opportunity, Ava, and when the email about the job came through, I thought instantly of you.'

It all seems rather Hollywood movie and not at all what I'm used to. I mean, I live in a two-bed flat in Brixton that I share with my mother and younger brother. I sleep on a sofa bed in the lounge at night and I work two jobs. Or I was working two jobs until I was fired from my cleaning job at a central London hotel last week — due to an error that wasn't mine, but that I got the blame for — and my work with Fairweather Childcare Solutions is inconsistent at best.

'But what *is* the opportunity?' Frowning, I flick through the pages of the NDA again but I'm none the wiser.

'I can't tell you that until you sign.'

'Why would I sign something before I know what it is?

For all I know I could be signing away a kidney or agreeing to become the front part of the human millipede. Or was it centipede?' I grimace as a thought hits me. 'Or even worse, the back.'

Nala pushes her floral-framed Cath Kidston glasses up her nose, a sign that she's nervous. Since I signed with the agency two years ago, Nala has been kind to me. She has a lot of experienced people on her books and her agency has a good reputation in the circles of London's upper middle class, but it's been hard for her to find me work because of my domestic circumstances and because of my other job. Though the latter won't be a problem anymore. 'You're not signing the contract itself, Ava, just a document to say that even if you decide not to go for the job, you won't tell anyone about it.'

'Oh.' I nod. 'I see.'

I'm pretty sure that Nala wouldn't let me become a part of a monstrous creature that eats... well, best not to think about that, but this job could involve anything. However, she has reassured me that I'm only agreeing not to discuss the job even if I don't want it, so it's worth a shot.

Nala chews at her full bottom lip then exhales slowly. 'Look, Ava, I know things are tough for you right now. This is an amazing opportunity for you to make a difference to your circumstances. I wouldn't bring it to your attention if I didn't think you'd be perfect for it. You're a solid, reliable employee. Children and parents like you. As you know, your issue with overnight stays and living in has restricted what we can offer you at Fairweather Childcare Solutions, but if you could just see a way to overcome that... in this instance, you'll be in with a chance of getting a job that will solve all your financial problems.'

I'm about to insist that I'm not having financial issues,

but Nala would know it's not true. My three credit cards, high-interest loan and rent payments take every penny I earn. With it being late August, I need to get Daniel's school uniform for the new academic year sorted quickly. I would have bought it in July when the stock appeared in the shops, but he's been growing so quickly that I was worried it wouldn't fit by September. I still intend on having a browse around the charity shops to see what they've got but he'll need the school blazer with the badge and a decent pair of shoes. The familiar twisting in my gut ensues as I wonder how we're going to manage. Thinking about money and how much I haven't got is my least favourite activity.

As if reading my thoughts, Nala asks, 'How's your mum?'

My eyes roam the small central London office that is stuffy with the early August heat, flickering over the plants on Nala's filing cabinets then to the window that overlooks a busy road. Opposite, is a building housing a flower shop on the ground floor, a cosmetic clinic on the first floor and a psychiatrist on the second floor. Some of the essentials for modern life together in one building, I think. You can celebrate or commiserate with the flowers, get a quick shot of Botox or filler then head to the shrink to chat about exactly what's going on in your mixed-up brain.

'She's... the same.' I cough to dislodge the painful lump that's risen to my throat.

'The same?' Nala raises her sculpted black brows slowly.

'No better. No worse.'

What else can I say? My mum, Nancy Thorne, has been unwell for so long that it's part of life. Once a talented seamstress making garments for some of the big fashion houses, she's now unable to work for long periods at a time and is limited to taking in alterations and repairs. Mum is only forty-eight but she relies on me to pay the rent and put food on the table. She *hates* relying on me, I know that, but she has no choice. If I wasn't around then she'd suffer and so would my ten-year-old brother, Daniel. They are my world and I'd do anything for them.

Anything at all...

'This job is amazing.' Nala holds out her hands, palms facing upwards. 'I wish I could say more but I can't until you sign. Can you trust me on this, Ava? You know I'd only suggest it to you if I thought it was worth it.'

Meeting her brown eyes, I make a decision. I like Nala and she's been good to me. As good as my circumstances would allow her to be. I know she would have got me more work if I'd been prepared to be a live-in nanny or to do regular overnight stays, but with my second job working evenings and some weekends, I couldn't commit fully. Now though, the only issue is leaving my mum and brother overnight. It would mean that Mum will have to get Daniel ready for school in the mornings and it's a lot for her with her health issues. Daniel is a good boy but he can be quite energetic and, like all children, demanding at times.

'You'd be able to pay someone to help your mum out while you were away.' She covers her mouth with a hand then shakes her head. 'See, I shouldn't have shared that part. I'm already telling you too much.'

'I'd be away? For how long?'

She sighs then says quietly, 'A few months.'

'A few months?' My voice wavers and my stomach drops like a stone in a pond, but then I steel myself. It's not like she was going to offer me an amazing job that was 10am to 3pm with weekends off. Who'd pay great money for a nanny during school hours?

'But, sweetheart, it's only temporary and you'd be allowed some time off for visiting, as well as some rest days.'

'So... let me get this straight... if I sign the NDA, you can give me all the information and I can still decline the job?'

'Yes.'

What have I got to lose?

'I place the paperwork on the desk, pick up a pen and sign on the dotted line. Never have I been more curious or more anxious about committing to something in my life. But if Nala's telling the truth and it means I can help my family, then I'm prepared to find out more.

Chapter 2

Ava

On the tube ride home, I hold the paper handles of the delicatessen bag tight. Perhaps it was foolish to splash out but after reading the full details of the job and deciding then and there to accept it, I felt the need to celebrate. In the bag are some of my mum's favourite things as well as some salmon for dinner and a delicious looking cheeseboard. I even splashed out on a bottle of elderflower cordial for us and a cloudy lemonade for Daniel. Mum will be worried when she sees the bag, but we never shop at expensive delis and it's a special occasion.

A woman in the seat opposite me glances at the bag then lower, and I see a tiny line appear between her brows. I follow her eyes and shame rushes through me as I spot what caught her attention. My toe is peeping through the hole at the front of my black court shoe like it's trying to escape. I stuffed a piece of cereal box there this morning and coloured it in with a black marker from Daniel's pencil case, but it must have moved and now my toe is there with its chipped varnish, peeping out like an anxious mouse. I adjust my legs, so my other foot is in front of the hole.

When I look up, the woman catches my eye and offers a sympathetic smile but I look away. Sympathy is hard to take when things have been so tough. Sympathy doesn't change anything at all. Only action can make a difference, make things better.

And I have taken positive action today. The knowledge that I won't have to wear broken shoes or worry about debt-collection threats again makes me want to dance around the carriage, swinging from the poles and singing like they do in musicals. After I signed the NDA, Nala put the job contract in front of me and the first thing I noticed was the amount the successful candidate would be paid. An amount I could never have dreamt of earning from one job. An amount that will pay off debts and give me money to put aside for Daniel's future and to get us a better home. I read the contract through carefully, trying to absorb the details but I couldn't get the amount out of my head. Nala did say that there was a caveat, that even if I accepted the job, the employer would need to do a background check on me first to ensure that I was suitable — even though I had all that done before the agency signed me — but I simply nodded along with a goofy grin on my face. If they, whoever *they* are, because that information wasn't on the contract, are prepared to pay me *that* amount of money for four months of my time, then I can't turn it down. It's a lifechanging sum and one I can't turn my nose up at.

So I signed. And now I need to wait and see if the employer is happy with what they find out. Nala seemed pretty certain that it would be fine and told me she's not putting anyone else forward for the job right now because she wants me to have it. Before I left her office, I gave her a hug because she has just given me the chance of a lifetime.

At my stop, I exit the train in a rush of warm air that

smells of oil and chips, and head for home, my toe sticking out ahead of me like it's showing me the way.

Chapter 3

Edward

'Eat up then we can go out in the garden.'

My four-year-old son, Joe, peers up at me from his plate of scrambled eggs.

'Can we play football, Daddy?'

'Of course we can.' I reach out and fluff his soft, blond hair and my heart squeezes. Everything in his world is about to change and he has no idea.

'Will you be in goal?' He chases a piece of egg around his plate with his small fork and I resist the temptation to help him. Sometimes it's frustrating because it takes Joe five times as long to do things as it would take if I helped, but he needs to be able to do things himself. In fact, he insists a lot of the time and if I don't let him do it... well... that's when I'm glad that Cynthia is there. Actually, I'm always glad that Cynthia is there, and I don't know how we're going to manage when she's away. Joe will miss her, and I certainly will. She's a reassuring presence, a stable pillar in our lives and the fact that she's going to be gone for four months makes me feel rather queasy.

My phone vibrates in my pocket, so I pull it out and swipe the screen.

'No phone, Daddy.' Joe shakes his head, his brown eyes wide.

I sense someone looking at the back of my head and I turn to find Cynthia has stopped loading the dishwasher to watch me. Even though we have a housekeeper, Cynthia still helps out with some of the domestic chores, especially when it involves clearing up after Joe.

My phones vibrates again and I hold it up. 'I have to take this. I won't be long.'

'It's Saturday, Edward.' Cynthia's tone holds a warning. She might be an employee but she doesn't hold back when it comes to my parenting. But then she's been around for a long time. Since I was a baby, in fact, and so she feels confident enough to speak her mind. Most of the time, I'm happy with this because it's good to have someone who's not afraid of me, someone who'll tell me the truth, but at times like this, when something's happening at work and I'm needed, it grates on my nerves.

'I'll be back before you finish your eggs,' I tell Joe, averting my eyes from his disappointed little face, then I leave the room and head for my study, ignoring Cynthia's sigh of dismay.

Closing the study door behind me, I take a deep breath and become Edward Cavendish interim CEO, leaving everything else behind me as I prepare to deal with business. As a father, I might have areas where I'm weak and uncertain, but as a businessman, I'm in my element because it's where I'm in control.

Chapter 4

Ava

My cheap new suitcase and rucksack stand in the hallway in front of the door with its frosted glass pane. There is a smell of damp in the hallway despite the citrus reed diffuser that sits on the narrow table beneath an oval mirror that once belonged to my maternal grandmother. My maternal grandparents are long gone, and I never met my paternal ones because my father's mother passed away when he was just eighteen and he didn't know his father.

I can barely believe that I am leaving today despite repeatedly reading the text message I received this morning instructing me to be ready to be collected at noon. A car is on the way to pick me up and that again made me think of Hollywood movies. In the space of less than two weeks, my whole life has started to change.

Daniel has followed me around like a shadow since I told him that I'd be going away for a while. There's a fifteen-year age gap between us and Daniel was a surprise baby conceived after one of my father's fleeting visits. We've always been close and I do more with him than Mum because her health issues prevent her from being more active, and that makes me worry. How will they manage while I'm away? We have no relatives around us and while the neighbours in the flats either side of ours are nice enough, they're not family.

'It'll be OK, love,' Mum smiles at me from the kitchen doorway. She has a tea towel in her hands and I can't help noticing how white her knuckles are as she grips it tight. Her pain must be bad today. The side-effects of the cancer treatment she received four years ago have lingered and the lymphoedema and fibromyalgia leave her exhausted.

'I hope so.' She opens her arms and I step into her embrace. She feels so small these days, like everything she's been through has shrunk her. 'You promise you'll eat properly?'

'I promise,' she murmurs into my hair.

'I've filled the freezer with meals.'

'I know.' She leans back to look at me. 'The cupboards are groaning with goodies.'

It's true. I went to the supermarket yesterday and did a big shop and I've arranged a weekly delivery slot for Mum and Daniel to get a regular restock. I've also set up some online subscriptions, so they'll get other essentials delivered during my absence.

'I've put that money into your account now and you have the emergency credit card?'

'It's safe in the drawer. Now stop worrying.' She pushes my hair behind my ears. 'Dan and I will be fine. With that games console you bought him, I doubt I'll see much of him anyway.' She laughs but I know she was worried when I took him to get one. Once I'd signed the contract, everything happened quickly. Nala phoned me three days after our meeting to tell me that the employer had completed the background check and was happy that I fit the criteria. A retainer was paid into my bank account that day and I kept looking at my balance to make sure it was still there. It was more than I could earn in a year with two jobs, and it was just a retainer! I knew I couldn't leave it sitting there though so I paid off some debts, transferred some to Mum and paid the rent for the next six months. After that, I'm hoping we'll be able to look for somewhere better to live and that thought has kept me going every time I've experienced a flicker of doubt about going away.

'Don't let him spend too long on it each day. It's meant to be a reward for doing his homework and helping out around here. I still wish you'd let me hire someone to come in and help.'

'Ava, the thought of having a complete stranger come into my home to cook and clean fills me with horror. I'd end up cleaning before they came and it would be more stress than it was worth. If things get too much, then I'll reconsider, but for now, I'm sure we'll be fine.'

'Don't worry, Ava, I'll help Mum.' Daniel has emerged from his bedroom and comes to me. 'I know you're worried but it'll all be fine. Perhaps when you finish your job we can go on a holiday?'

The hope in his voice almost undoes me. We've never been able to afford a holiday. He's talked about them a lot after his school friends told him about theirs and I know there have been some school trips he would've loved to go on but our budget just couldn't stretch to it. Things will be different after this contract is done though. For sure.

'Of course we can. I'll be back before January for visits but we can definitely talk about a holiday.' Wrapping my arm around his shoulders I pull him close and kiss his brown hair. He comes up to my shoulder now but he's still very slight compared to some of his friends. I love him so much I want to wrap him up in cotton wool and keep him safe from the world but I also know that he has to discover things for himself. Mum and I will do what we can to help him to navigate his way through life and money will really help with that. After all, the new uniform I wanted to get him is now in his wardrobe, washed and ironed, as are the shiny black shoes he needed and the trainers for when he has physical education lessons. He's all ready to start the new term at school. Sadly, I won't be there for his first day back, but I guess everything comes with a price.

'Don't be sad,' he says, giving me a tight hug. 'Go and enjoy your new job.'

My mobile buzzes in my pocket and I pull it out and see a message from the driver. He's outside so it's time to go.

I swallow hard and kiss Daniel again then pull myself away. After I've hugged Mum one final time, I go to the door and open it then pick up my luggage.

'I love you both so much. I'll let you know when I'm there safely.'

Mum smiles and Daniel takes her hand, letting me know that he's the man of the house now.

Then I step outside into the August sunshine and head towards the black car with tinted windows that's waiting on the road, preparing myself to embark upon this new adventure.

Chapter 5

Edward

Name: Ava Marie Thorne
Age: 25
Height: 5 foot 4 inches
Hair: light brown
Eyes: amber

I read through the profile the private investigator sent me again. There are more details like her education background, where she lives and her work experience to date, but it's the photographs that interest me most. Ava is... well... pretty average, I guess. Not too short or too tall. She tends to wear her hair tied back and very little makeup. She's curvy but it's hard to tell how curvy because in the photos I've been sent she's wearing large T-shirts that could even be men's and those baggy boyfriend jeans that were fashionable a few years ago. Could still be fashionable for all I care. All that matters about Ava, really, is that she's as unlikely as a unicorn. She's a rare creature because she doesn't have any social media presence at all. Well, except for an old Facebook account that she hasn't been active on for over ten years. She's exactly what we needed but I can't help wondering if she sounds too good to be true. I guess time will tell.

I close the file on my iPad, drop it on the bed and gaze out of the bedroom window. Joe is running around the grass while Cynthia pegs washing on the line that's off to the side of the house. It's the perfect picture of domesticity and she could easily be his grandmother. We could easily be a normal family with normal concerns and a normal life. But we're not. We live in this massive house that my earnings paid for in the beautiful Buckinghamshire countryside. My father, Peter Cavendish, passed away when I was twenty-one and my mother, Helen, lives in Scotland with her second husband, so Joe has no grandparents around him. My only other surviving relative was my grandfather, the founder of Cavendish Construction of which I am interim CEO, and he passed away six months ago. Grandpa, otherwise known as Silas Cavendish, was a workaholic who clung to his job title until he took his final breath. Only then, after working my way up from the bottom after graduating university, was I allowed to take over and, until the Board of Directors vote next year, there's no guarantee that the title will be mine permanently. Grandpa saw to that, stubborn and cantankerous old man that he was.

And so I rattle around the enormous family home that my wife and I chose together when she was pregnant with Joe, with my son and our staff. There's the housekeeper, Polly Treharne, Cynthia, who's our nanny, and her husband, Laurence, who manages the grounds along with his team. We have cleaners but I rarely see them so well are they managed by Polly. In fact, I sometimes feel like we have ghosts that come in and clean around, a fact I don't share with Joe because he's already sensitive about what happens when we're no longer here. And no wonder, poor boy.

A few years back, I was enjoying my life, thinking how lucky I was. I seemed to have it all... a beautiful wife, adorable baby, a successful company that would one day be under my control and a grand country house. Then everything changed. A sour taste fills my mouth and I go to the ensuite and swill my mouth with cold water straight from the tap. I learnt the hard way that life can change in an instant, people can turn out to be very different to the version of them you believed in and happiness can be destroyed. I splash some water over my face then pat it dry with a towel, attempting to ground myself with physical sensations before the spiralling starts. But it's too late and my mind is gripped by the familiar thoughts.

I was a fool to give my heart to someone because people die. People lie. People... are people — flawed, foolish, ungrateful, deceitful, disloyal.

Never again will I put my trust in someone else. I'm in this for my son and for myself now and the rest of them can go to hell.

Shaking it off, I return to the bedroom and consider heading out to play with Joe. It would make his day. Young children are such simple creatures, wanting time and attention far more than money or gifts, and yet I know that these are the things I struggle to give to Joe. It's easy to buy him things and hope he'll understand that it means I care, whereas being with him is more complicated. I try, I really do, but spending time with him brings so many memories back. It's easier to leave him in Cynthia's capable hands and retreat to my study, to bury my head in paperwork and online meetings and things that have no power to hurt me.

If I was psychoanalysing myself, I'd probably believe that my attempts to distance myself from Joe lie in my fear of caring about people. It hasn't got me far in the past other than into painful predicaments where I've been made to look like a fool, where I've been hurt beyond measure.

And so, instead of going outside, I pad down the stairs to my study and close the heavy door behind me. There will soon be a new nanny here to learn the ropes from Cynthia and to care for Joe. It's time for me to go back to the city, to mingle with my peers and employees in person again, to secure my role as CEO before someone else swoops in and steals it from under me. I have been working from home but I've physically buried myself in the countryside for two years and I need to return to civilisation and make my presence felt. While Grandpa was alive I could get away with hiding but now, if I want to prove to the board that I can be permanent CEO, I need to return.

I also, rather annoyingly, need to find myself a new bride fairly soon because the clock on that issue is ticking faster every day. Dear old Grandpa and his bloody Bridgerton style marriage clause that states I must be married by thirty-five in order to inherit his shares in Cavendish Construction and to become permanent CEO. I swear that when he had the clause written into his will in the weeks before his death, he wasn't of sound mind. I know that I could question the clause but it won't make a shred of difference because the Board of Directors is made up mainly of his old chums, and even if legally the will could be overturned, his chums will ensure that his final wishes are carried out. Why the hell didn't he tell me before he died to give me the chance to change his mind? When I heard the clause at the reading of the will, I almost keeled over myself. Grandpa was a majority shareholder so if I don't inherit his shares, the company will become a completely different beast. His shares could be divided and sold to different people or bought by one person who'll change Cavendish Construction forever. I can't let that happen.

Thanks, Grandpa, for making my life even more difficult. And thanks for putting me in a position where I could lose the one thing that has been constant in my life: the family business.

Chapter 6

Ava

The car that's been sent for me is a black Mercedes Hybrid which is so shiny I can see my reflection in its exterior. I fight the urge to get my brush out of my bag to try to tidy up my hair which I curled this morning and which already looks like an unruly mess.

The driver is an older man, probably in his late fifties, wearing a smart black suit with a matching tie. He introduces himself as Jeff Turnbull while my mum and brother look on, then he takes my luggage and puts it into the boot. I stand there awkwardly, not sure what to do because I rarely ever take a taxi anywhere, using the bus or train instead. Deciding to appear helpful, I follow him around to the back of the car but he's already turning back so I run straight into him and bounce off then stagger backwards, arms flailing. I manage to regain my balance and look at him but his face is a serene mask of professionalism. I guess he deals with clumsy young women like me all the time.

When he opens the back door to the car then stands back, I realise that I'm meant to get in, so I do. He closes it gently then goes around to the driver's side door. He starts the engine and my stomach somersaults. This is really happening.

'May I open the window?' I ask. 'So I can wave goodbye.'

As if by magic, the window goes down without me doing anything, and I wave at my mum and brother, my heart aching as I gaze at their faces for the last time in weeks or even months. We can videocall, of course, but I know it won't be the same as seeing them every day.

You're doing this for them, I remind myself sternly, *so pull yourself together*.

'On the seat is a box for you from your new employer,' Jeff says.

'Oh...' I glance at the box. 'Thanks.'

The car pulls away from the kerb and I wave at my family until we reach the end of the road and they disappear from view.

To distract myself, I return my attention to the box. There is a card taped to the top, so I reach for it and slide my thumb under the flap. I pull it out and read.

Dear Ava,
Your agency provided all the necessary details we needed but we are very much looking forward to meeting you in person.
Inside the box are some essentials for you to use during your employment. You'll find all the numbers you need already in the phone and the iPad is connected to the cloud so you can access documentation regarding your employment. As you know from the contract you signed, you are

not to access social media accounts from either device — or any other device — during the period of your employment. Should you do so, your employment will be immediately terminated, and any outstanding monies will not be paid.
Enjoy the journey and relax.
Kind regards,
Cynthia Beaumont

I put the card back in the envelope and place it to one side then open the box. Inside I find the equipment the letter referred to and I look at it for a moment. Don't get me wrong, I knew what I was letting myself in for in terms of social media blackout, but see, that didn't matter to me at all. I only have one Facebook account and I haven't accessed it in years and as for the other socials, well, I've avoided them like the plague. I know that's unusual and what some people see as weird, but for me, I had good reason not to want to see what was going on in the world in that way. I watch the news when I have time and sometimes read the headlines, but all the rest of it, well, there's always a chance it will bring up some information about *him,* and I simply don't want to know. You can't cause that much hurt and devastation and expect people to carry on as if they haven't had their hearts broken and their world turned upside down. While my friends at school were creating profiles all over the place, I was avoiding being seen, hiding away from visibility and it seems that it has paid off.

'Everything all right back there?' Jeff asks. 'Would you like me to close the window for you and put the aircon on?'

Meeting the Billionaire Boss

'That would be great, thanks.' I smile at him in the rear-view mirror and he nods.

'Anything you need or want to know, just ask. Apart from that, try to relax and enjoy the ride.'

'Thanks.' I smile again even though his eyes are now on the road ahead.

My mind wanders back to reading the contract in Nala's office. It was all very official sounding and Nala talked me through the details she'd received. The employer wanted to find a nanny for his young son to cover a period of time while the long-term nanny is away. I have no idea where she's going but the contract is for four months. During this time, I'm to be available throughout the week and over weekends, but breaks and days off can be negotiated depending on the employer's schedule. Seeing as how I'm going to be away from home, this all sounds fine to me. I've received more information since then and it turns out that the employer is named Edward Cavendish and he's an interim CEO of a big English construction company. He lost his wife two years ago and there was a lot of social media coverage because they were one of those 'it' couples, always splashed over the tabloids and Instagram, according to Nala. The wife was a successful French lingerie model and had a body, Nala said, that she could only ever dream of having. Anyway, they had a baby, and he was only two when he lost his mum and it all sounded very tragic and I felt my heart filling with sympathy for the man and his son. How awful to lose the woman he'd thought he'd spend his life with and who was also the mother of his child. Nala said the trauma of it all is why Mr Cavendish is so against social media. He doesn't want his son having his privacy invaded and so the contract stipulates this and the terms must be adhered to at all times. Not only that, but the nanny must aim to avoid any situations where the child could be captured on camera. As someone who hates being photographed, I have no problem with this.

And now, as I sit on the seat made of soft, buttery leather and gaze at the iPad and iPhone in the box, I know that I will never do anything to jeopardise the boy's privacy. I pick up the phone and swipe the screen and it invites me to add facial recognition, which I do, then I flick through it, checking the numbers in *Contacts*. I see Mr Cavendish's number there.

Edward, I touch a finger to his name then jump as it dials him and so I end the call quickly. *Edward Cavendish*. Nala said he reminds her of the actor Chris Pine and so this is who I imagine as I put the phone back in the box along with the card then put the lid back on it.

The journey takes just over an hour and a half but it feels like minutes because I'm so comfortable in the car. There is even a small fridge in the back that contains water and fruit juice, and Jeff tells me to help myself to a drink. I take a bottle of water but I only sip it because I don't want to need the loo before we get there.

Jeff stops the car outside ornate, wrought-iron gates and waits until they swing inwards then he drives us along a winding road that takes us between well-established trees and past several houses that he tells me belong to Cavendish employees. When the red brick house comes into view though, my breath catches in my throat because it is enormous, like something out of one of those period dramas Mum watches on TV. It is seven bays wide and has three storeys below a cornice and parapet with smaller windows in the attic. Large, flat lawns border the driveway that leads in a circle around what I think is an actual sundial. Wait until Mum sees it, I think, experiencing a pang of sadness that she's not here with me to see it all right now. Knowing that I would be going through a background check, I was ultra-careful not to Google Mr Cavendish or his home or family. I didn't want to be found at fault in any way, and somehow, searching for them online felt like it would be invading their privacy. And this is why I'm in shock as Jeff pulls up in front of the stately home.

And why, as he comes and opens the door for me and I step out, I feel like I'm going to be completely out of my depth.

Chapter 7

Ava

A woman, who I find out when she introduces herself is Cynthia Beaumont, opens the large, black front door as I climb the steps. It's as if she was waiting there all morning for me to arrive. Her hair is short and red, and as I get closer, I can see that it's flecked with white. She's smartly dressed in black trousers and a white blouse and wearing flat black brogues. I wonder if I'll need to wear a similar sort of uniform or if I'll be allowed the freedom of my own clothes. I picked up some cheap white T-shirts and stretchy jeans when I did the big food shop at the supermarket because my clothes were getting pretty threadbare, but now I'm wondering if I should have paid a bit more. Nala told me that Mr Cavendish was rich but I had no idea that she meant *this* rich, although the very generous salary should've prepared me, I guess.

Cynthia leads me inside and as I look around, I have to force my jaw closed. The hallway is enormous with a staircase that sits at the centre then splits into two that lead off to the left and right of a mezzanine landing. It has one of those fancy dark red carpets with golden swirls and brass rods across the back of each step to hold the carpet in place. The ceiling is ornate with cornices and a chandelier hangs above my head. Off to the right and left are doorways, and I can see from here that they lead into rooms with high ceilings and large windows.

'Ahem.' Cynthia clears her throat and I lower my eyes to meet hers.

'Sorry. I... I've never seen anything quite like this.' I rub at the back of my neck.

'Take them up to her room, Jeff,' Cynthia says and I turn to see the driver standing in the doorway holding my luggage. I'd clean forgotten about my belongings as I came inside like some naïve debutante at her first society ball.

Jeff nods then climbs the stairs and disappears off to the left of the staircase.

'It's quite something, right?' Cynthia smiles warmly and the tension in my shoulders loosens a fraction. 'I have to be honest though, after working for the family for thirty-three years in houses exactly like this, I tend to forget how magnificent my surroundings are.'

'You've worked for the family that long?' I ask, appraising her. She's slim and toned and has good skin. It's pale and freckled and although she has some fine lines around her olive-green eyes, I wouldn't have thought she was more than fifty.

As if reading my mind she says, 'I came to work for them when I was twenty-nine.'

I do a quick sum in my head and my surprise must show on my face.

'Yes, I'm sixty-two now. I can hardly believe it myself.' She laughs. 'Anyway, Ava, it's very nice to meet you. As you'll know from the information given to your agency, I'm Joe's nanny. I live in, well... I actually have a house on the estate with my husband, but I do stay some nights when Ed — I mean Mr Cavendish can't be here and also when I'm needed. My husband and I used to live with the elder Mr Cavendish, Edward's grandfather, but when Edward bought this property with his wife, we moved here. He's a very kind and generous employer, you see.'

'Where does the older Mr Cavendish live now?' I ask.

'Silas Cavendish passed away six months ago. He left his house and estate to the National Trust because his son is dead and his daughter-in-law lives in Scotland with her second husband. He knew Edward didn't need, or want, his estate, but he did leave the family business in his charge.'

'I see.' I swallow, trying to digest this information to process it all later. Imagine having an actual estate that the National Trust would want. This family must be loaded.

'I'm here for the next week to help you settle in then I'm going away on a four-month trip of a lifetime. My husband and I are heading off to celebrate our 30th wedding anniversary.' She sighs. 'It's not easy for me to leave Edward and Joe — I find it hard referring to him as Mr Cavendish because I was his nanny too — but my husband and I always talked about this trip and I think that if we don't do it now then we might never do it. So... I really hope that you'll be all right here and that you'll take good care of Joe.' The concern on her face makes me reach out and touch her arm.

'I will, I promise. I'll treat him like he's family.'

She lifts her chin and smiles at me. 'That's exactly what I needed to hear. Right then, let me show you around. I won't give you the full tour because that would take a while...' she laughs, 'but I'll show you to your room and the rooms you'll use the most.'

'Lovely.' I realise I'm still touching her arm so I remove my hand and tuck it into my pocket.

Cynthia gives me a quick tour, showing me my room with its ensuite complete with walk-in shower and clawfoot tub, as well as a large four-poster bed and a window overlooking the lawns at the side of the house. It's like a fancy hotel room and I can't believe I'm going to be staying here for four months. Then she takes me along the hallway to Joe's room, which is slightly smaller than mine with a window looking out over the rear gardens and an adjoining door that, she tells me, leads into Mr Cavendish's room. I stare at the door with its wooden panels and heavy handle and feel a blush creep into my cheeks. There's something intimate about knowing that his bedroom is right next door, and that when I'm here with Joe, Mr Cavendish could be just the other side of the panels. It's a strange situation for me but one that I'll probably soon get used to.

After that, I'm shown the lounge, the drawing room and the kitchen which is right at the back of the house with a large open fireplace, a six-foot wooden table and so many cupboards I think I'll need to label them, so I don't forget where everything is. But then Cynthia introduces me to the housekeeper, Polly Treharne, a rosy cheeked, shapely woman with blonde hair in a neat bun and an easy laugh that brings a smile to my face. She places her hands on my arms, peers at me then pulls me into a hug that squashes me up against an ample bosom and tells me not to worry, that I'll soon settle in. She asks what I like to eat and drink and if I have any allergies then explains that she oversees the cleaning staff and does most of the cooking, although from time to time, Mr Cavendish likes to cook himself, so he gives her the evening off.

My head is spinning when I climb the stairs to my room to unpack. Cynthia has told me that I'll meet Joe tomorrow after breakfast as he's currently out with his father, and that

I should rest before dinner which we'll eat in the kitchen at eight. I'd half hoped to meet Mr Cavendish on arrival but also, for some reason, the thought makes my stomach churn. Perhaps it was because Nala kept on about how handsome he is or perhaps it's because I've barely had anything to do with men over recent years — apart from those I encountered in the hallways of the hotel and one of Daniel's teachers, although he wore a wedding ring — but whatever it is, I'm sure I'll soon get over it. After all, Mr Cavendish is going to be paying my wages and so our relationship will be nothing but professional. I'm sure even I can handle that.

Chapter 8

Edward

Entering the lobby of our central London building is strange. On one hand, it feels like I've been away for ages and on the other it's like I've never been away. The security guards on reception are familiar and they stand up and greet me respectfully. I raise my hand in a wave then walk on towards the lifts, my shiny shoes tapping on the even shinier tiles as I go. Although I'd never admit it to anyone, my heart is racing, and I don't want to talk to people. The need to get to my office and close the door overrides my conditioning to be genial and polite. That can wait because right now the last thing I want is to see pity in people's eyes. I don't want pity. I want to be me, getting on with my life, back at the top of my game. I've hidden away for long enough and now it's time to get back to business. Not being here in person hasn't been great but I have continued to do my job remotely, as have many people since the pandemic, and until six months ago, Grandpa was still working, still ruling over the business with an iron fist. But with him gone, the responsibility falls on my shoulders and now it's time to prove that I can become the permanent CEO of Cavendish Construction.

The lift carries me to the penthouse where I have my office and I take the time in the enclosed space to breathe deeply, slowing my heart right down, self-soothing in the way I have learnt. The man I was before would be shocked to see me now, would be horrified even, at how everything has impacted upon me, but then the old me hadn't lost his wife in a horrific car accident and nor did he have a young son to provide for. A young son who relies on me to love and care for him. The weight of responsibility lies heavy on my shoulders sometimes and I wonder if I can ever be enough to fill his mother's shoes. How can one man be both father and mother to a child and create the balance he needs to grow into a well-rounded individual?

I've been a businessman for as long as I can remember, even as a child I'd ask Grandpa questions about how his construction company worked and beg him to take me to his office so I could learn more. It's like I was born to do this and it's where I thrive, overseeing projects, negotiating deals, working alongside my best friends and colleagues, Jack Kendrick and Lucas Barrett.

The lift door pings open and I step out onto the floor and head for my office. My PA, Darla, knows I'm coming in today, but I told her I wasn't sure what time. Her desk is empty as I pass it and I exhale a sigh of relief because I was hoping she'd be at lunch or in the gym, which is one of her favourite places to frequent. *Or was...* It's crazy that I've been away for two years. Yes, I've been working from home but returning here was something I tried to do several times and simply couldn't face. People told me it was grief and shock and that time would heal my wounds, that grieving is a process that takes as long as it takes.

To be honest, I'm not so sure I'm healed. More... holding myself together with a business suit and tie, wearing them like armour as I try to resume my life again.

I can do this, I really can. I should have done it sooner but there was much to sort out and then there was Joe and time just flies. Not to shy away from the fact that I couldn't get out of bed for the first six months or so because I could barely breathe. I think Grandpa kind of saw my grieving as weakness and it made him doubt me, made him think I was more like my father than he'd previously suspected. Grandpa loathed what he saw as weakness and after what happened to my father, I can kind of understand why. But I also think that he was wrong about emotion being a weakness and I know that suppressing feelings is bad for you. I tried and look where it got me. Grandpa was from the generation of the stiff upper lip, of gritting your teeth and getting on with things, no matter what. Unfortunately, his parenting style probably led to my father's issues and his need to numb himself with drink and drugs. I was lucky in that I had my mother, to a certain extent anyway — because Mum always seemed a bit distant, like she was waiting for a chance to get away — and, of course, Cynthia. That woman has been a rock for me and I owe her my life.

But I've done it. One step at a time. And here I am, back in work. Ready to be the mogul I was meant to be.

Closing the door behind me, I cross my office to the window and gaze at the incredible view. London glows golden in the late August sunshine. Familiar landmarks stretch out for as far as I can see and the Thames snakes its way between buildings and under bridges, a murky mirror of the sky. The sight calms me and I know that I've done the right thing coming back and that this is the right time. I can and will slide back into my shoes, or at least become a new version of me, scarred beneath the surface but appearing the same outwardly.

There's a rapping at the glass door and turning to the sound, I see two familiar faces. I wave them in and they approach me, arms wide and I hug them in turn.

'Looking good there, Cavendish,' Jack pats my back hard as he hugs me then steps back to let Lucas do the same.

'He's definitely lost muscle mass,' Lucas says with a grin as he squeezes my biceps. 'Not the hunk he was.'

'Piss off, Lucas.' I make a grab for his stomach. 'What've you got there? A regular food baby, you silver fox.'

Lucas feigns horror and pulls his shirt from his trousers revealing rock hard abs. 'You're mistaken Cavendish. I take good care of myself.'

Laughing, I nod. 'You both look great.'

We sit on the sofas in the corner of my office and they fill me in on what's happened recently. It's nothing I don't already know as they kept me in the loop throughout my time away — we've had regular online meetings, as well as nights in drowning my sorrows, but it's not the same as speaking to them in person practically every day. While we speak, I feel myself relaxing, the familiarity of the workplace and my friends, who are like the brothers I never had, comforting me. It feels good.

'So what's up with you?' Jack asks, rubbing a hand over his thick light-brown beard. Along with his tattoos, it makes him look like he could fit in with a motorcycle gang. 'Didn't you say something about Cynthia going away for a while soon?'

'Yeah...' I grimace. 'She's off on some anniversary trip. Could've done without it to be honest but she's been there through everything, and I could hardly deny her this, could

I? I don't know how I'd have managed without her these past two years. Or before that.'

'Who's going to look after the little one?' Lucas leans his arms on his thighs.

'I have a new nanny starting today. It's only temporary and she'll leave when Cynthia returns.'

'A new nanny, eh?' Lucas wiggles his eyebrows. 'Details, please.'

'Don't go there.' I laugh. 'Anyway, she's not your type.'

'What's that supposed to mean?'

'You know what I mean. You like your lady friends straight off the catwalk.' Lucas has a penchant for models although I've yet to see him out with any of them for more than a few dates.

'I'm picky but I can afford to be.' He's joking and I know he is. I also know that he's a commitment phobe, and he has good reason to be with his painful past. But then, don't we all?

'What's the nanny like?' Jack asks. 'Just so we don't say the wrong thing when we meet her.'

I rub at the back of my neck. I wasn't there when she arrived yesterday and I avoided her when I returned home then I left early this morning to hit the gym in London. Before coming to the office, I grabbed brunch as a way of easing myself back in. Of course, I know I'll have to meet her soon, but for some reason, I'm not in a rush.

'Well... I had her vetted and she's some kind of social media hater who lives with her mother and brother and... from what I've read... works her ass off for minimum wage.'

'I take it you made her an offer she couldn't refuse?' Jack raises his eyebrows.

'I'm paying her a salary that should drastically improve her life, yes.'

From the moment I knew that I'd need someone to cover for Cynthia, there was never any question in my mind about scrimping on childcare. This woman will get a salary that will, hopefully, make her apply herself one hundred per cent to taking the very best care of my son. As well as keeping her head down and her mouth shut.

'But is she hot?' Lucas asks so I shake my head.

'For fuck's sake, man. Is that all you think about?'

'I'm guessing she is the way you're being so cagey about it.' Lucas sits back and folds his arms over his chest. 'Can't *wait* to meet her.'

These two men are integral to my existence. We've been through thick and thin, have had each other's backs since we met at Oxford. They say that blood runs thicker than water, but with us, it's more a case of friendship runs deep. I'd do anything for Jack and Lucas, and I know they'd do the same for me. Which is why this ribbing is fine, it's all part of our relationship, a guy's (kind of twisted) way of showing that we care.

'Look,' I say finally, 'she's OK. She's nothing flashy and definitely not a supermodel but who wants a hot nanny, right? She's there to care for Joe and nothing else.'

'So, she won't be tucking you into bed at night?' Lucas winks at me.

'Absolutely not.'

'Speaking of being tucked into bed... what about the inheritance clause?' Jack's question makes me groan and I bury my head in my hands. 'Isn't the clock ticking?'

'It's ticking,' I reply, a sinking feeling in my stomach.

'Isn't there anything you can do to change it?' Lucas tilts his head, a fine line between his brows.

'You know how it works with the Board of Directors. Grandpa's ghost will haunt his chums if they don't vote the way he wanted. I have to find a bride before I turn thirty-five if I want to be CEO and majority shareholder.' Repeating the terms doesn't help them sink in at all; I think I'm still in a form of denial.

Lucas shakes his head. 'Seems pretty unfair in light of what you've been through.'

'Him changing the will in his final weeks was a shit thing to do but I can't change his mind now, can I? If I'd known before he passed away, I could have tried to speak to him about it but when he did ask if I'd marry again, I told him I never would. I guess that just pissed him off. Silas thought that being married was better for business in terms of networking and for the family reputation and so now I'm stuck with this stupid clause. It's embarrassing.'

'Your grandpa encouraged you to adopt the good old stiff upper lip then?' Lucas grimaces.

'Stiff-*up-a* something.' Jack shakes his head. 'You need to find a bride, Edward. Shame he didn't just write that you had to get married regardless of your spouse's gender because I'd sweep you off your feet and then you'd be sorted.'

'If only he'd been less specific, right?' Groaning, I shake my head, although I'm not sure how I'd feel about marrying Jack…

After my father's untimely and rather lonely death when I was just twenty-one, Grandpa became even harder than ever. I think seeing his only son alienate his wife, squander money on gambling and drink himself to death must have broken his heart. In a strange way, the clause makes me think he was looking out for me but it's archaic and unfair and so I can't feel entirely sorry for the old man. He hid the severity of his illness well and he must have known the end was coming, which was why he had the clause state that I had to marry before I was thirty-five. My birthday is in May and so time is running out if I want the board to approve my position. Otherwise, who knows what interloper will end up in charge of the family company?

'But brides don't just grow on trees, do they?' I state the obvious.

Jack and Lucas fall silent as we contemplate the thought.

'It's not like I even want to date, let alone marry. After losing Lucille like that, the thought of committing to another woman just turns my stomach. Besides which, how can I find a bride who'll love my son like he's her own and in less than nine months?'

Of course, I was married and way before turning thirty-five, and Grandpa seemed happy about that. But now... I'm a widower. I hate that word so much because of the air of tragedy it carries with it. Finding someone and falling in love with her in less than nine months sounds crazy, in fact, downright impossible because after Lucille died I swore I'd never fall in love again. And I'm pretty certain that no woman will ever be good enough to be a mother for Joe. No woman could ever measure up to what I want for him.

'Well, the way I see it,' Jack says thoughtfully, 'is that you should start by getting back on the horse.'

'The horse?'

'In the saddle. Well, on a woman. You know how the saying goes. We need to take you out and get you back into the swing of socialising again. You never know who you might meet.'

'This isn't a regency courting season, you know.' My tie suddenly feels too tight, so I stick a finger between it and my throat and yank it away.

'It's true that it's a circus out there.' Lucas grins. 'But we can at least have some fun while you do some window shopping. I know you've been through hell but you're still young. We'll start tonight.'

'I can't. Not tonight.'

I think of Joe and Cynthia, then of Ava, wondering how she's settling in and if she's nervous about starting her new job. It looks like she's led a quiet life so far. It also looks like she's worked hard for years supporting her family and I find that admirable. With her lack of makeup and her understated clothes, she's not at all flashy, and yet... the more I think about her and those photos of her I browsed on my iPad, the more I want to find out. She deserves a chance to enjoy her life. Without the salary I'm paying her, it could have taken her years to make things better for herself and her family. If she'd ever have been able to with the cost-of-living crisis. And if she deserves a chance to enjoy her life then can I truly deny myself the chance to do the same? Besides which, my best friends want me to be happy and snubbing their efforts seems harsh. They don't deserve to have to keep propping me up. Two years is a long time to support someone the way they've supported me.

'Of course you can,' Lucas says as he stands up and tucks his shirt in. 'Let the new nanny and Cynthia get to know each other without you standing over them. Cynthia's a tough old bird but you can be an intimidating bastard so give the new nanny a chance to find her feet without you glowering at her.'

'I don't glower!' I scowl at Lucas then realise what I'm doing so make an effort to relax my brow.

'Yeah, right.' Lucas shakes his head. 'You can go back tomorrow evening and find out how they're getting on. And, in the meantime, we can grab an early dinner and some drinks then hit a club or two. You'd be surprised how therapeutic it is having a pair of long, shapely legs wrapped around your waist or a pair of glossy lips wrapped around your co—'

'Enough!' I raise a hand and my eyes flicker to Jack, hoping that he'll counter what Lucas is saying but he's nodding along.

'Be good to get you out again,' Jack says.

And just like that, I know I've been cornered. Tonight will be one of those nights when I'm at the mercy of my wingmen.

As we head for the lift, I find that I'm actually looking forward to it.

Chapter 9

Ava

It's been a strange day. For so long my life has involved getting up and helping Daniel get ready for school then heading off to one job before going to the other. On my days off, which were rare, I spent time with Daniel and Mum, cleaned the flat, daydreamed about the kind of life I could have had if I'd been born into a different world. Watching those property programmes on TV, I'd envy the people who had insane budgets of eight hundred thousand pounds to spend on a dream home. How did people manage to find that much money to spend on a house and, when pressed, stretch higher to get the property they really wanted? They had enormous open-plan kitchen diners with bifold doors that opened onto beautiful gardens; they had sofas in all colours, plush rugs and open fireplaces or log burners that would make any cold, winter's night cosy. They had four or five bedrooms, at least two bathrooms, and those deep, free-standing baths that tempt you to sink into them and relax. The list of all the things that were out of my reach went on and on.

No longer it seems. Or at least not for now because this

house is incredible. And as long as I stick to the contract, I'll have money when I finish my time here. I'll have the money to make a difference to Mum and Daniel's lives.

This morning, as promised, I met Joe when Cynthia introduced us in the garden. He gazed at me from behind his thick eyelashes, his brown eyes curious, but his body language suggested that he was reserving judgement until he got to know me better. Cynthia told him to shake my hand which he did then he asked her if he could go and play. As he ran off to the impressive wooden climbing frame with slide and swing, I felt a pang of homesickness. Not for the flat but for my family. And yet, it made me feel for this small boy who had lost his mum and was about to spend four months without the woman who had taken care of him and been there since the day he was born.

'I'm going to miss him,' Cynthia had said as we watched him on the slide, a hand straying to her throat as if the pain was too much. 'He's a good boy.' She turned to me then and met my eyes. 'But I have a feeling he'll be fine with you.'

'He will,' I said, sounding surer than I felt. I was already warming to Cynthia and wanted her to feel that she could trust me with her charge. 'I'll take good care of him.'

She nodded. 'I probably shouldn't say this but... would you keep an eye on Edward too?'

I swallowed to hide my surprise. I had yet to meet my employer.

'He's been through such a tough time and he... he needs people to look out for him too. He might be a big, strong man but he's vulnerable. He won't admit it, but I know how he's struggled. He was a sweet boy and I've had the pleasure of seeing him grow up, but no one ever thought things would go the way they did. Losing Lucille was a terrible blow and it broke my heart seeing him suffer. But...' She took a deep breath. 'He has, at last, gone back to the office in London so I'm hoping that finally he's turning a corner.'

I was aware that Mr Cavendish had gone back to London early this morning. I had to confess to being a bit disappointed that I wouldn't meet him yet, but it did give me the chance to have a look around the house and to find my bearings. This was something I really needed to do because the house was enormous and put the properties on the TV shows into the shadows.

After I met Joe, Cynthia told me to take the day to settle in. Before lunch, I wandered the grounds, admiring the green lawns, the orchard, the giant greenhouse that was filled with a variety of fruits and vegetables. There were also raised beds and a herb garden and I crouched down and plucked a sprig of thyme, crushing it between my fingers and enjoying the rich herby scent. Mum grows herbs on the kitchen windowsill but there isn't room for many and I know how she'd love the herb garden and the Cavendish house. I could picture her strolling in the gardens, perhaps picking herbs that would help with some of her ailments, eating freshly grown organic produce rather than whatever was cheapest at the supermarket. Daniel would be able to run and play without us worrying about cars and pollution, the fresh air and good food would help him to grow tall and strong. In that moment I wished with all my heart that they were there with me.

When I returned to the house, I walked around for a bit, acquainting myself with the ground floor. Cynthia had told me to stay out of Mr Cavendish's study but that I could feel free to check out the other rooms. I passed the door to his study, wondering what it was like inside but resisting the urge to take a peek. Instead, I went to the next door, and, to my delight, I found a library. The room was bright and airy, with two sets of French doors opening out onto the rear garden. Heavy red velvet curtains were held back from the windows with twisted gold satin ropes with tassels. The bookshelves went from floor to ceiling and I browsed the shelves, admiring the selection of books from early hardback editions to modern thrillers and romances. For a bookworm like me, it was like walking into heaven and I knew that I'd enjoy spending time in this room. There was a dark brown leather recliner near the French doors so I decided to take a moment while it was quiet. I selected a book, a contemporary romance with a bold and colourful cover, took it to the lounger then sat down and made myself comfortable.

My initial reservations about sitting down and doing nothing other than relaxing soon faded away as I got lost between the pages. It was a wonderful way to while away the morning and I couldn't help thinking that I could get used to this.

Chapter 10

Ava

Three days later, I'm in the garden with Joe. He's still wary of me, but with Cynthia's support, we're getting to know each other. He likes playing outdoors, so I make an effort to play on the climbing frame with him, even going on the slide while hoping that my bottom doesn't get stuck. I find his enthusiasm and energy infectious and when he suggests that we go further into the gardens to be explorers, I agree.

At the one side of the garden are stone steps that lead down to more perfectly manicured lawns. Either side of the steps are grassy slopes and at the top of one, Joe and I lock eyes. Instantly, I know what he's thinking. It's a beautiful August day with a gentle breeze and the grass is dry, so I think, *why not?*

We lie down on the grass and then I go first, rolling from the top of the slope to the bottom. The world spins around me and I experience a sense of freedom that I haven't felt in quite some time. Joe giggles all the way down the slope and we do it again and again. After the fifth time, we are both red cheeked and gasping, so we sit at the top of the slope together to catch our breath.

'That was fun,' Joe says to me. 'I like you, Ava.'

'I like you too, Joe.'

His smile lifts my heart but I hold back from wrapping an arm around him. I want him to be able to trust me and to be happy spending time with me, but I also know that children need time to get to know people when they enter their lives. Joe is young but he's been through a lot and so I will take my time to earn his trust and build a relationship that he feels confident about. Until now, Joe's world has been small, his time spent mainly with his father, Cynthia, Polly and Jeff. Cynthia said he's been to nursery in the mornings but it's a private nursery that is part of the school he'll be attending and that they keep the numbers low.

'Shall we do it again?' I ask. 'Just one more time though because we have to go and wash our hands before dinner.'

'Yes, please!' He grins then lies down and I do the same.

'Ready, steady... go!' I shout and off we roll.

At the bottom of the slope, I lie there, gazing up at the flawless blue sky, and when a small hand creeps into mine, I squeeze it gently.

'What's going on here?' A deep voice makes me start. I sit up and instantly my cheeks flood with heat.

There are three men standing at the top of the steps staring down at us. Suddenly self-conscious, I scrabble to my feet and help Joe up too. I'm aware that my jean shorts and white T-shirt are creased and as I look down, I'm horrified to see that there are grass stains on my T-shirt and it has risen up exposing the skin of my belly.

'Daddy!' Joe tugs his hand from mine and runs towards the man standing in the middle who scoops him up and hugs him.

'Hey Joe.'

'We're rolling down the hill like bales of hay,' Joe says.

'I could see that.'

The man who I now realise is Mr Cavendish returns his gaze to me and if it's possible, my blush deepens. The more I think about how red my cheeks are, the hotter they become. I must look like such an idiot and he's probably regretting hiring me already. He is impossibly good looking with thick dark hair and a neatly trimmed beard. His eyes are so dark brown they seem black — so it registers with me that he's unlike Chris Pine in that respect — and I can't help noticing how his white shirt hugs broad shoulders and that his strong forearms dusted with dark hair are exposed by his rolled-up sleeves. He has the appearance of a man who works out and takes care of himself. There's an expensive-looking watch on his left wrist and his trousers are slate grey, fitted like they're tailor made, which I suspect they are.

'Aren't you going to introduce us, Edward?' The man to his right asks and I look at him, taking in his golden-brown hair and matching beard, light-brown eyes and the tattoos on his arms. These men look like they've stepped out of the boardroom and into a period drama and I feel incredibly awkward and incongruous.

'I haven't been introduced myself yet,' Edward says, his eyes slipping down my body and pausing for a moment at my midriff so I tug my T-shirt down but that pulls it taut across my breasts and when his eyes rise, I see them widen slightly. 'I take it that you're Ava?'

'Yes.' I hold out a hand but realise that he's too far away to shake it, so I climb the steps and stand in front of the men, feeling small and vulnerable.

Edward shifts Joe to one hip then takes my hand and squeezes it. A jolt of electricity shoots up my arm making me gasp. When I meet his eyes, I see that he's frowning as if he felt it too. Or it could be a frown of disapproval and that thought makes me wish the ground could swallow me whole.

'Good to meet you, Ava,' Edward says, easing my discomfort slightly. 'These are my friends and colleagues, Jack Kendrick and Lucas Barrett.'

Jack takes my hand first followed by Lucas. They are both attractive, Jack making me think of a rockstar with his bushy beard and tattoos and Lucas has that George Clooney sexy grey hair thing going on, but neither of them evokes the spark of electricity that Edward did. It also occurs to me that they are older than me, not much but around nine or ten years. They most likely think I'm a naïve idiot, a girl without a clue about the world. In some ways they'd be right.

'Can I have a drink, Daddy?' Joe asks.

'Of course. You go on up and I'll be right behind you.'

Edward sets Joe down and he runs towards the house, his blond hair ruffled by the breeze, his small legs jogging him from side to side.

'We should head up and prepare for the meeting,' Jack says, nudging Lucas.

'What meeting?' Lucas frowns but Jack bobs his head at me. 'Oh... yes... Of course.'

They walk away, tall, broad-shouldered men in their expensive clothes with their expensive watches and their expensive educations. They are well spoken, confident in their own skin, from a world I could never be part of in a million years.

'How are you settling in?' Edward asks, and I meet his brown eyes again.

'Very well, thank you.' I'm conscious of how I have to

crane my neck to look up at him so I take a step up to stand on the path at his side. But even there, he still towers over me.

'Do you have everything you need?'

'Yes, thanks. You have a lovely home.'

He nods. 'It's not bad, I guess.'

We both look towards the magnificent property, its windows glinting in the sunlight. Jack and Lucas are standing near the French doors of the library now, their heads close together in conversation.

'It's wonderful. Especially the library.'

He raises an eyebrow. 'You like to read?'

'Very much. I've used the local library in Brixton regularly since I learnt how to read as a young child, so living in a house with its own library is a dream come true.'

Am I gushing? I am. I'm gushing like a fan backstage at a Harry Styles concert.

He nods. 'Well feel free to read any of the books you like. And please encourage Joe to read too. He likes books a lot and it's something I want to foster.'

'Of course.'

'Right then... if you need anything, don't be afraid to ask.'

Suddenly, he reaches out and touches my hair and my breath catches in my throat.

What's he doing?

My knees go weak. My mouth goes dry. My lips part.

He brings his hand back and shows me. 'You had grass in your hair.'

'Oh!' I run a hand over my ponytail, realising that my hair must be in a state. Looking down at myself, I see the grass stains, accepting that I'll have to bin this T-shirt because there's no way I'm getting them out.

'Ask Cynthia if she has something for the stains. Joe has a habit of getting dirty so I'm sure she has something there that'll work.'

His eyes linger on my T-shirt a fraction too long and my heartbeat quickens. Was he looking at my breasts? Again?

Of course not! I admonish myself. Just the mess I've made of my top. I'm sure he thinks I'm a right mess and could well be considering firing me at the earliest possible opportunity.

'Thanks for making such an effort with Joe,' he says. 'Cynthia's a bit past rolling down grassy inclines so he'll have enjoyed that.'

'I enjoyed it too.'

'You looked like you did.' There is mischief in his eyes now. 'Are you going inside?'

'Yes. I need to change before dinner.'

We make our way up to the house and I try to ignore how good his cologne smells as the breeze carries it to me as well as how handsome he is. This man is my boss and I have no right to see him as anything else. It will only lead to disappointment and could ruin this incredible chance for me to change my life. I haven't wanted to be with a man in ages and that's not going to change now just because I felt something when my skin met his.

Nothing is going to happen between us. Our relationship is strictly professional.

But however much I want to, I can't deny that Edward Cavendish is incredibly hot.

Chapter 11

Edward

The day has worn on and the sun is low in the sky, bathing the horizon with a soft peach glow. After dinner, which was eventful as Jack and Lucas ate with us — and by *us*, I mean Cynthia, Joe and Ava — and they were clearly enjoying themselves far too much showing off for Ava's benefit, we went through some paperwork then came outside to the terrace.

'It's a gorgeous place,' Jack says. 'That view is spectacular and it's so calm and quiet.'

I nod. Being here has helped me over the past two years, even though there are ghosts around every corner. Lucille loved this house and the gardens although I never saw her rolling down a grassy banking with Joe. Lucille said that there was a lot she wanted to do to this house but with her frequent modelling trips, pregnancy and then her death, she never had the chance.

'Life is a rollercoaster, right? But being outdoors can be so beneficial.' Lucas swirls brandy around in his glass then stares into it as if it has the answers to the meaning of life.

'I wish my father had realised that,' I say, surprising

myself because I don't speak about him often, not in any detail anyway. 'But he had issues he didn't understand and his relationship with Mum was challenging at the best of times. They should never have married but Mum was pregnant, then... after they married, she lost the baby.' I don't add that this was due to an argument that escalated and ended up with Mum falling down the stairs. She only told me about this recently and I was horrified. My parents' marriage wasn't just tense, it was volatile. It wasn't a good example of how to live happily ever after. 'They stayed together and I came along but they were never happy. I don't know if Dad's behaviour was worse because they were together or if his behaviour made things worse between them. Whatever way around things were, they weren't well matched.' By *behaviour* I mean my father's drinking, use of drugs and womanising. As well as his gambling that got him into masses of debt and that Grandpa had to bail him out of many times. Jack and Lucas know a lot about my background but there are some things I don't share. Some things are too dark to say out loud.

'So your grandpa believed that marriage to a good woman will keep you on the straight and narrow?' Jack asks.

'I guess so.' I shrug. 'Or at least he thought so at the end.'

Neither of my friends says that I *had* a happy marriage. They know the truth about that too. Although, it was happy for a while, and I did adore Lucille. Until things went wrong.

'But what if you marry and it isn't happy? What if it became toxic too?' Lucas drains his glass then sets it on the table. 'There's always a chance. It's easy to fall in love but also easy to fall out of it.'

The three of us are similar in that we've been through difficult times. I thought I'd found the one. Jack did too, once upon a time. As for Lucas though, he's never found a woman he wants to settle down with. At least that's the story he's sticking to.

'That's why I'm thinking that a marriage where feelings aren't involved might be for the best. After what happened before... my heart doesn't have the capacity to go through loss again but if I married someone for convenience rather than love, then there would be no chance of me getting hurt.' The seed of this idea has been lurking at the back of my brain for a while and the more I think about it, the more sense it makes.

'Kind of like a business arrangement.' Jack nods his approval. We all like good, clear deals where there's no room for error or confusion, where costs and overheads are laid out at the start and there's no room for movement. Contracts go through negotiations, everything is signed and sealed and off we go.

'So you need to find a bride who'll be happy with that.' Lucas snorts. 'I don't think any of the women I know would go for it. They all seem to want the fairy tale.'

I sip my brandy and hold it in my mouth then enjoy the gentle burn as I swallow. 'But for someone who needs a good deal, it might work. For a woman who needs something I have. Like money that would change her life.'

'Would you be happy having a marriage that was only in name?' Jack runs his hand over his beard. 'Without any of the other benefits of being married?'

'You're talking about sex, right?' I down the last of my drink and pour another then offer the bottle to Lucas who fills his glass then Jack's.

'Of course.' Jack nods. 'Sex is important. But also... it would be a marriage without any intimacy at all.'

'That would suit me better this time around.' My tone is

sharpened by a bolt of pain that pierces my chest out of the blue. 'I can get sex anywhere. I'm not interested in love or emotional intimacy. I just need a wife so I can inherit the majority of the business for me and for my son and to secure my position as CEO.'

At that moment, I glance towards the house and there, framed by the open French doors of the library is Ava. Her hair is down, falling in chestnut waves over her shoulders and she's wearing the plain black shift dress and strappy sandals she changed into for dinner. Her shapely legs are bare from the knee down and earlier I noticed a tiny birthmark on her right ankle that reminded me of a lightning bolt. She's young, and although I didn't think so when I first saw the photographs of her, she's pretty too, in a natural way. From her looks to the way she carries herself, she is the polar opposite of Lucille.

When her eyes meet mine, her lips part slightly then she smiles and raises a hand. I incline my head then turn away, not appreciating the way my heartbeat has quickened or the way something seems to be happening lower down. It's been a long time since I had sex and for someone who once needed it regularly, it's been strange. But grief and pain can do that to a man, like an unwelcome form of libido suppressant.

As well as a wife who lies.

Inwardly, I shake the thought away.

'What about the nanny?' Lucas asks and I see that he's looking towards the house. 'She seems pleasant enough and might appreciate a contract involving cash.'

'She's young though,' Jack says. 'She probably wants a loving husband and a family.'

I shrug as something occurs to me. 'I'm not averse to having more children. If we both knew exactly what the deal was then she could have all that. And I'd be a good provider.'

'You changed very quickly then from not wanting emotional intimacy to being prepared to have sex and children.' Lucas laughs. 'It seems our Cav has got a thing for little Miss Ava.'

'Piss off!' I roll my eyes, but I can't help wondering what Ava would think about the idea if I asked her. 'Anyway... she needs to settle in here before I make any... indecent proposals.'

My friends laugh then we refill our glasses and gaze out at the horizon, watching as peach turns to lavender then endless black as another day comes to a close. When I turn to the house, I see that Ava is no longer in the library and my heart sinks a little.

Is it possible that my future bride could already be living under my roof? Is it wrong that I'm hoping so?

Chapter 12

Ava

The first day of the September school term arrives and I'm up early to get little Joe ready. Cynthia is leaving today but she wanted to be here this morning to see him off. Dressed in his grey shorts, white shirt and stripey tie, he's so cute that my heart aches. Since my arrival, we've spent more time together and we're getting on well. He's a sweet boy and has accepted me into his life. The transition could have been difficult but having Cynthia here while he adjusted has been helpful. I can only hope that he'll be all right after she's gone but I'll do everything in my power to make sure that he's happy.

Cynthia told me that Joe did attend the school's nursery and that he's been to a few transition days at the reception class, so we're both hoping that he'll soon get used to his new routine.

At eight o'clock we gather in the hallway. Cynthia and I fuss around Joe, checking he has everything he needs for today then Edward takes some photographs on his phone. I ask if he'd like some of him with Joe and he nods then hands me his phone. I take lots, wanting to capture this precious moment for them but I can't escape the feeling that they're missing out on something. Or someone. Joe's mum should be here too, eyes glistening, a proud smile on her face as she watches her baby prepare for his first day. I wonder briefly if having a nanny around for her baby was strange but then probably not as many upper middle class people have hired help.

When I go to hand the phone back to Edward, our fingers touch and the spark I felt before when we first shook hands shoots up my arm again. Is this man walking around in shoes that create static or is it something else? If the brush of his skin against mine does that to me, what would happen if we got closer? Shaking the thought away, I return my focus to Joe.

'Have a good day, Joe.' I offer him a big smile.

'Thank you, Ava.' He smiles back and relief fills me that he's relaxed and happy about what lies ahead.

Cynthia wipes at her eyes with a tissue she procured from her cardigan sleeve. 'I guess I should get ready to leave too.'

'You're going to have a wonderful time.' Edward smiles at her.

'I think so. Laurence is very excited and I am looking forward to it although I will miss my boys.' Her eyes slide to Edward and he shakes his head.

'Go and enjoy yourself, woman. You deserve to have a fantastic holiday. Also, I've upgraded all your flights to first class so you can travel in style.'

'What?' Cynthia gasps. 'You didn't!'

'Of course I did.' Edward's smile is broad but I see something else in his eyes. Is he going to miss Cynthia too? From what I've learned about them, they are close and very fond of each other. She's been a mother figure to him and to his son. I don't know much about his own mother, but I have a feeling that she's not around very often, which seems a shame as Joe could benefit from having his grandmother nearby. I'm certain that if my mum was a grandmother, she'd be there for her grandchildren despite her physical limitations. She's a wonderful mother and would be a wonderful grandmother. I hope that one day she gets the chance to be a grandparent. Mind you, it will probably be with Daniel's children as I have no desire to be in a relationship at all, and it's kind of necessary to have some contact with the opposite sex in order to procreate. Unless you use a sperm donor, of course, but if I ever did decide to try to have a child, I think I'd prefer to do it the old-fashioned way.

'Thank you, Edward.' Cynthia says then she steps forwards and wraps her arms around him.

Not wanting to interrupt this moment, I walk quietly to the doorway, already thinking of the list of things I need to get done today. Keeping busy and being productive will help pass the time until Joe comes home from school, and I want to prove that while I'm not Cynthia, I can be helpful and useful. Who knows, if I impress Edward and Cynthia enough, even after the contract ends, there could be more work available for me.

Edward and Joe pass me and descend the steps to the car that Jeff has brought round to the front. Jeff opens the back door and helps Joe to get onto the booster seat then fastens the belt around him while Edward gets in beside him. Cynthia has followed them, and she hands Joe his small rucksack and his sun hat and hugs him one final time.

As Jeff drives away, I am holding it together until Cynthia turns and climbs the steps and I see the tears in her eyes. She presses a hand to her mouth as she tries to stop herself from breaking down but when our eyes meet, it's too much. I hold my arms out to her and we hug, our breath coming in shattered gasps as we try to regain our composure.

I'm finding it hard to accept that there are some things I can do and some that I can't. Not that I physically can't do them but there are people employed here to do them. Cooking meals and cleaning are off the menu. The same with washing and ironing. There are staff employed to do those things and I find it so strange. I'm used to sorting my own washing and stuffing my own dirty clothing into the machine with a non-bio detergent and fragrant (if cheap) fabric softener. But here, I've been told to leave my washing in the basket in my bathroom and that someone else will take care of it.

And so, my first day without Cynthia or Joe around has been a strange one. Desperate to appear useful, I've tidied Joe's room, put his clothes in his washing basket and also made his bed. While I was in his room, I could hear a deep voice in the adjacent room. After he returned from dropping Joe at school, Edward told me he'd be working from home for the morning. He was speaking to someone on the phone in his room and I couldn't make out what he was saying (not that I was trying to because I'm not a snoop) but from his tone, I gathered that it was most likely a business call. That's something I have noticed about my boss. He's always busy. If he's not playing with Joe, he's exercising or entertaining his friends or working. Mostly working. The light in his study is on late into the night and when I've opened my bedroom curtains a few times in the mornings, I've seen him returning from a run or a bike ride. He's an energetic person and never seems to stop. Cynthia hasn't told me anything deeply personal about him but she did say that he's had a difficult few years, and is only now emerging from the grief of his loss. I can understand how keeping busy helps him to deal with things. I've always been the same. Being busy helps me to avoid thinking about my father and how angry I feel about his behaviour.

When four o'clock comes, I find that I can't wait to see Joe. I want to hear all about his day and to help him with his homework before settling him for the evening. After Edward left for London this afternoon, and Cynthia went off on her trip, it was just me, the silent cleaning staff and Polly, but she was busy in the kitchen. I didn't like to disturb Polly so I found myself wandering the house searching for something to do. It's a lot harder keeping busy than you'd think so I decide to speak to Edward and ask him what he'd like me to do in the hours when Joe is at school. At least then I can't get into trouble for not pulling my weight.

When I hear tyres on the gravel driveway, I run to the door and throw it open. For now, my charge is home and I am ready to give him my undivided attention. Everything else can wait.

Chapter 13

Ava

The last week of September has arrived, and the landscape is changing. The shades of green are giving way to yellow, red, orange and brown, and the weather has cooled. The orchard is abundant with ripe fruit, and I wander down there every day to pick some for Joe's lunchbox and to eat or use in baking. Polly has told me that I can use the kitchen whenever I like and so I have, which has been a relief as it offers one way to use my time. When I did broach the subject of what Edward would like me to do during the school day, he waved a hand and told me to use my time wisely, which didn't help, so I decided to use my initiative. Joe likes my apple muffins, and the apple and blackberry crumble I made him at the weekend and I have lots more recipes I'd like to try.

It's hard to believe that I've been here for five weeks now but I do feel that I've settled in, and my surroundings no longer feel strange. Edward has also given me a car to use while I'm here and it's so beautiful that it's taken me a while to get used to having access to it. I passed my driving test at eighteen but purchasing a car seemed beyond my wildest dreams and I've been reliant upon buses and trains all my life. But now, I have the use of a brand-new metallic blue Audi Q4 e-tron. More than once, I've found myself sitting in the car, admiring the sleek interior, the amazing sound system and the sheer size of it. If anyone had told me a year ago that this was where I'd be, I'd have laughed them out of the room.

During my time here, I've taken a wander around the house to admire the portraits of Edward's ancestors that hang on the walls. Polly said that Edward inherited them from his grandpa. They clearly date back hundreds of years and while I don't know who the people are, I make up stories about them. There's one overlooking the hallway of a man wearing what I think is a regency suit with a black cutaway coat, tall standing collar, white shirt, waistcoat and a ruby cravat. His leather breeches are tight and reach his boot tops. He has dark hair like Edward's and thick, black brows that frame his fathomless eyes. I've nicknamed him *Mr Darcy*. He looks very stern, so I imagine what has happened before he posed for the painting and more than once, I've wondered what Edward would look like wearing that outfit and I have to confess to finding the idea quite arousing. With his broad shoulders and the muscular legs that I've seen when he's wearing his running shorts, I'm certain that he'd look good in regency clothing.

The house has many rooms, most of which are unused and look like they haven't been decorated in decades. Furniture sits under dust sheets, bulky white shapes like ghosts of a forgotten era when the house would have, presumably, been busy. I wonder if Edward brought all of the furniture to the house or if some of it was left here by previous owners. At first, it made me sad to see the unused rooms, to wonder what it would have been like when people sat on the chairs, used the piano, slept in the beds, but now I'm getting used to the sense of emptiness that exists in some areas of the house. The quiet is soothing and so different from life in Brixton where there's always noise and bustle.

The bedrooms at far corners of the different wings, where curtains hang either side of sash windows, and where my footsteps echo as they tread boards that haven't felt the weight of a human in months or even years, are fascinating. Who slept in these rooms? Were they young or old, happy or sad? Did they have hopes and dreams that were realised or did they spend their lives feeling unfulfilled? It's a shame that so much of the house isn't used and yet, how would Edward fill these spaces? With family? With guests? If the house was sold, then I can imagine it could be divided up to create luxury apartments or taken over by a trust that would turn it into a tourist attraction. Perhaps it would even be used for TV dramas and movies as some similar properties are now.

Yesterday, as I kneaded bread dough on the kitchen table, I asked Polly about the house and she told me that it's been like this for as long as she's been here. The previous mistress, Edward's wife, had plans to redecorate and renovate, but she was so often busy with her career — apparently she had to travel a lot for modelling jobs — that finding the time to oversee such projects was difficult. And then, after she was gone, Edward lost all interest in doing anything at all to the property.

When I told Polly that I'd like to use more of the fruit from the orchard for making jams and preserves, she told me that there might be jars and other useful equipment in the attic. Apparently, nothing gets thrown away when you have plenty of space to store it just in case it's ever needed. I decided then and there that I'd go and explore today after Joe had gone to school. And so, here I am, climbing the staircase on the second floor that leads to the attic.

Standing outside the door, I feel anxious. Only having lived in a ground floor flat, I'm not used to having access to an attic and this one doesn't even need a ladder, it has actual stairs. The doorknob is brass and feels cool to the touch and a shiver runs down my spine. This could be a horror movie and the audience could be shouting at me right now, telling me to turn back and ignore my curiosity. But, of course, that's for movies and make-believe and this is real life. The worst I can expect to encounter up here will probably be spiders and possibly bats. I'd prefer not to come across either one but they're infinitely preferable to an axe wielding murderer or a poltergeist of some kind, or even a vampire that will drag me into the shadows and feast upon my blood. Sometimes I think I might have read too many books...

The handle turns with a groan and the door squeaks on its hinges as it swings inwards. The vast space before me is filled with hazy light that enters through the paned windows, creating rectangular patches on the floorboards. The way the light falls creates areas of shadow and those are the ones that make the hair on my nape rise. Anything could be hiding there, ready to pounce, ready to swallow me whole.

'Cut it out!' My voice emerges shakier than I'd like but I needed to hear something other than the pulse of blood through my ears. I am an adult, and I am perfectly capable of exploring an attic without getting the jitters. 'Now where would the jars be stored?'

There is a clear pathway through the middle of the attic while on either side, beneath the windows, are piles of things. Some are covered with dust sheets as in the bedrooms below, and I get the sense of forgotten eras as I walk past them. Time has stood still here for many, many years and I decide to come and have a good look through things at a later date — after I've checked with Edward if it's OK to do so, of course. There could be old toys here that might interest Joe and possibly family photographs that he'd like to see. The more I get to know him, the more it becomes clear that he's a bright and inquisitive child and he deserves to be educated about his family background, to know the mother he lost. I'm sure he'll have questions as he gets older and there might be answers in this attic.

When I reach the far end, I realise that starting there is probably foolish. It's more likely that recent items would be stored closer to the door, so I'll head back that way and begin there.

The first dust sheet I lift reveals a set of designer luggage, a Moses basket and a bottle steamer. The latter must have been Joe's when he was a baby and as I take a closer look at the luggage, I see that it is monogrammed with L.C. *Lucille Cavendish?* Curiosity drives me to pick up the one case and it's heavy. Are her things still inside? That thought makes me shiver and I put the case back where I found it then move on.

The next pile has some of those large plastic storage tubs with lids and so I crouch down to look inside them. There are baby clothes, some toys and one filled with photograph albums and something I haven't seen for a while... DVDs. It hits me then that I haven't seen any photographs around the house. There are portraits, yes, but they're years old and not of anyone still living. Have they been hidden away because Edward couldn't bear to look at them?

Before I can change my mind, I pull the tub away from the others and lift the lid, reaching for the photobook with *Joe* on the cover.

Chapter 14

Edward

This morning I had an early meeting in London and I intended on staying at the office for the rest of the day, but by early afternoon, I was restless. September is a month that I've always enjoyed. It goes back to school time, I'm sure, the sense that it was a time for new beginnings, fresh starts and all that type of thing. I was always happiest at school because I knew what to expect and when I was there, I could avoid my father's dark moods and my parents' arguments. Weird how a month that's near the end of the year can feel like that but this year, I felt it even more. Perhaps it has to do with Cynthia going away and having Ava around.

Ava seems to have settled in well and despite my initial reservations about having a new nanny in my home, I do feel quite comfortable around her. She's quiet and efficient and it's already clear that Joe adores her. Quite often, I'll get home to find them playing in the garden or sitting together on a blanket spread out on the grass, eating fruit from the orchard, and reading. One day, I went out to them to see what had captured Joe's attention and I saw that Ava had found some of my old childhood books in the library and was reading them with Joe. Not wanting to disturb them, I sat at the table on the terrace and feigned interest in my phone but I was watching and listening to their easy way with each other. It was funny to see the familiar covers of my old books again and to realise that some of the themes are still so relevant today.

As of yet, I haven't broached the subject of a marriage of convenience with Ava. It feels kind of ridiculous. How can you ask someone, an employee, if she'll enter into a business marriage with you? A marriage that will be in name only. A marriage that will enable you to inherit your family business and become CEO but offer her no love or intimacy, just a pleasing financial package that could change her life and that of her family? I'm not a cold-hearted bastard. If I was, this would probably be a lot easier. If I was, I'd marry someone from my social circle and be done with it, but the thought of being married again makes my chest tight. And surely most women I know would want more than I can offer and that's why it has to be a business deal and nothing more. Although I don't want to admit it, there is part of me that's terrified of being married again, of putting myself in that position. And yet I know that if I don't find a bride, I stand to lose everything.

Stupid bloody clause!

And so, I am biding my time, waiting for the right moment to speak to Ava. Being around her isn't hard, though. She's kind of growing on me, if that makes sense — her easy smile, her pretty face (yes, the more I see her, the more I find myself attracted to her) and how she is with Joe. It all makes me want to be at home more. Home was where I hid myself away for two years, a place that felt gloomy and empty at times, but a bolthole where I could escape the world. But now, the house seems different. Ava is only one person, but she seems to fill the house with light and hope.

Shit, I must be getting soft as I age.

And that must be why I find myself entering the house earlier than usual and pausing in the hallway to listen, to see if I can hear Ava's voice as she talks to Polly or as she sings while listening to music, her earphones in so she's oblivious to the fact that others are around her. That has happened more than once, and I've found myself stopping to listen as she sings. She has an awful voice, but I like it because there's something so raw and real about her belting out Annie Lennox, Shania Twain or Whitney Houston. She's more real than a lot of the women I've encountered in my life and in those moments when she's unaware that she's not alone, her unguarded freedom makes me want to know more. So many people put on masks to go about their daily lives, never letting anyone see behind the polished façade — hell, I should know because that's what business is all about — but Ava is different, and it does something to me that I've never felt before.

There *is* music as I stand in the hallway, loosening my tie, but it's not music that fills my heart with joy. Instead, it makes my stomach lurch. I follow the sound, the muscles in my shoulders tensing, my jaw clenching, the black cloud that had been receding as the weeks passed catching up with me again.

Chapter 15

Ava

Sitting on the floor in front of the large TV in the snug, I know I should turn the DVD player off, but I can't. It's like when you know you shouldn't stare at a car crash but your eyes search out the scene anyway. Something about human nature makes us curious and now I've started watching this, I can't stop.

The box in the attic was filled with albums and DVDs and I've gone through some of them in the hope there might be something nice there for Joe. But this one is of Edward and Lucille's wedding. I didn't even know that people still had wedding DVDS made anymore but then I guess it makes sense so they can keep a physical copy and not just a digital upload. Also, the DVD player being there was just too convenient to ignore.

Sitting cross-legged in front of the TV, I watch as Edward and Lucille glide across the screen. The band (yes they had a proper band) plays Christina Perry's *A Thousand Years*, which was announced as their song, and as they dance, they look deeply in love. I've never felt that and watching the newlyweds now makes my heart ache. Not just for me and for what I haven't experienced but for Edward and his bride, for what they had and lost. This was, of course, before Joe came along. Before they knew they'd become parents and before they knew what lay ahead of them. They are innocents. Unaware of what was to happen. And their innocence is both wonderful for them and yet so terribly tragic.

I raise my hand to my face and wipe at my cheek. It comes away wet. I am crying and it's something I rarely do. Since I was a teenager, I've told myself that crying is a waste of energy, that it gets me nowhere, and so I swallow tears back, suppress rising emotions, fight the weakness inside me that sometimes surfaces. I have to be strong and stoic, it's the only way to survive.

The song comes to an end and the wedding guests applaud then others join them on the dancefloor. There's Lucas and Jack who both have beautiful women on their arms; long limbed, golden tanned, shiny haired women wearing expensive dresses and shoes that would feed my family for years. After the men pat Edward on the back and kiss Lucille on both cheeks, they twirl their dates around the dancefloor and the camera pans in and out, capturing what must have been a truly magical day.

'What the fuck do you think you're doing?'

I freeze. *Oh no. Please no...*

I turn the TV off then turning, I see Edward standing in the doorway. I didn't hear him come home and now he's caught me watching this.

'I uhm... I...' His face is etched with pain and fury as if the emotions are battling for precedence. Pushing to my feet, I wipe my now clammy hands on my jeans. 'I'm sorry. I was looking for jars in the attic and I came across the box of

DVDs and thought there might be something here that I could share with Joe.'

His dark-brown eyes are filled with fury and my knees start to tremble. I've done wrong and now I'm going to lose my job. Mum and Daniel will be so disappointed and, oh my god, I'll have to leave little Joe. The thought of not being there to read to him, play with him and tuck him in at night is just dreadful. In the time since I arrived here, I've become so fond of him and I know he already relies on me. The poor child has been through enough change. What will happen to him now?

'What made you think you had the right to snoop around?' Edward's voice is like thunder as he comes closer to me and I back away, feel the TV screen against my bottom.

'I wasn't snooping, I promise. I'm so sorry that I've upset you. That was never my intention. What you've been through...' I raise my hand as if to touch his arm but he looks so angry that I'm afraid that if I do touch him then, like a wild animal, he might snap. He's bigger than me. *So much bigger.* And he's strong. I can see that from the muscles in his arms, the breadth of his shoulders, the ease with which he runs for miles across the land. It's something that even now, in this moment of fear at how upset he is, I find attractive. Edward is so masculine, so much more of a man that anyone I've ever met before.

He stops close enough to me that I could raise onto my tiptoes and kiss his lips. The thought makes my breath catch and I break eye contact, look down at his chest that heaves with emotion.

'I should've asked you if it was OK to watch this DVD.' My voice is soft, my body language submissive. I'm not naturally submissive to men but I have a lot to lose, and I don't want to anger Edward even more. And he's right, I shouldn't have looked through his things. 'I'm so sorry.'

When I raise my eyes to his face, his expression has softened, the anger gone like a passing storm cloud. My vision blurs and I blink to clear it.

'It's... it's all right. Just... check first next time, Ava, please.' He sighs like he's exasperated by an annoying and disappointing employee, rubs a hand over his hair then turns and leaves the room.

Every cell in my being wants me to run after him to see if he's OK but I know that he needs some time alone to process what just happened. Besides which, I am an employee, not a friend or equal in his world. That thought is both reassuring and somehow painful. I could never be with Edward in the way that Lucille was on that dancefloor. She was a model, confident in her beauty and elegance, whereas I'm... me. I know I have value as a person but to people like Edward and Lucille, I'm someone they employ to care for their children or their ageing parents. They don't see people like me as potential partners. I might be naïve in some ways but I'm not stupid. I know how things work in the world and Edward will only ever be my boss.

But as I eject the DVD from the machine and place it safely inside its case, I can't help thinking that it's all so unfair. I'm as good as any other woman on this earth. I might be poor, I might not have an Oxford education or ever strut semi-naked along a catwalk but I'm hardworking, caring and compassionate. I'm no great beauty, perhaps, but I'm all woman.

Just not to Edward Cavendish. There's no way on this earth that a man like him would ever look at a woman like me and truly see her value. I might as well be invisible.

Chapter 16

Ava

For the next two days, I barely see Edward. He's gone early in the morning and returns in the evening to say goodnight to Joe then disappears into his study like a bear retreating to a cave. I find it hard because I upset him with my thoughtlessness. I had sensed that we were getting on well, as well as a boss and employee could do anyway, and while I know I'd never replace Cynthia, I still wanted to be a valuable addition to the family for the duration of my contract. But now I'm worried I've ruined it all.

On Friday afternoon, while Joe is having a snack in the snug and watching a nature documentary — he's fascinated by them and Cynthia told me he's allowed to watch some TV in the evenings once his homework is done, and on Fridays after school he can have more time seeing as how it's almost the weekend — Edward finds me in the kitchen.

'Ava.' He nods at me as he enters the room and goes to the fridge and gets a beer. 'Want one?' He holds it out towards me.

'No thanks. I'm still on duty.'

'You can have a beer, you know. If you want one.'

'I'm OK thanks.' I continue folding the towels I've brought in from the line despite Polly's protestations about it not being my job. I need to keep myself busy.

Edward unscrews the top of the bottle then throws it into the recycling tub next to the bin. He seems awkward, unsure of himself as he leans against the cupboard and sips his beer.

'I meant to speak to you sooner about this, but tomorrow, Joe has a party.'

'Oh?' This is news to me. I have an app on my phone with his schedule and everything that's added to it appears there for me and for Edward, including things like parents' evenings, playdates and medical appointments. 'It's not on the calendar.'

'I know. It's my fault. I forgot to add it. Look... I can take him. It's no problem if you have something else planned. Or you could take the day off if you like.'

I meet his brown eyes and see the shadows beneath them. 'You've had a busy week.'

He shrugs. 'Lots to do. Some meetings that overran. An awkward client. Just the way business goes.'

'Would you like me to take Joe to the party so you can rest?'

He licks his lips. 'Not really. I mean... I need to go. It's a party for the son of family friends who we also do some business with from time to time. The boy is turning five and he and Joe have known each other since they were babies. Therefore, it's important that I show my face but... uh... I'd really like it if you'd come too.'

For a moment I get a flicker of something inside. He wants me to accompany him to this party. But then the flicker is doused as my common sense reminds me that I am the nanny, and of course he wants me there to look after Joe. It will probably be one of those parties where the children play and the adults talk business or make deals or whatever it is the upper middle class do to get on in the world.

'I'll come. Of course I'll come.' I smile primly then fold the final towel and place it on top of the pile.

'Thanks.' He takes another sip of his beer. 'It's an outdoor event so if you could make sure that Joe has a hat and a waterproof coat, just in case, that would be great. We'll leave at two.'

'I'll be ready.'

He walks to the door then pauses. 'Ava?'

'Yes?'

He holds my gaze, something going on behind his dark eyes, but then he sighs and shakes his head. 'Never mind.'

He's gone before I can respond, leaving me with a sense of frustration although I can't really pinpoint why.

Chapter 17

Ava

The next day, I get Joe dressed then Polly watches him in the kitchen while I get ready. My hair was a state so I washed and dried it then moisturised my face and put some lip gloss on. I emptied my wash bag on the bed to see if I had anything in there but apart from an old mascara and tube of concealer, it was empty. I threw them in the bin, deciding that it didn't matter anyway. After weeks of spending time outdoors with Joe, my skin is lightly tanned and my freckles more prominent across my nose and cheeks. It would take a barrel of foundation to cover them so there's no point trying. No one's going to be looking at me anyway so I'd just as well not worry about trying to enhance my appearance. I dress in a pair of navy cropped jeans and a white cotton blouse that I picked up in a charity shop. It still had the label on it so hadn't been worn and is cool and floaty, so it seems appropriate for the mild September day. I put a cardigan in my bag just in case then slip on my navy pumps and head downstairs.

I blow a kiss at Mr Darcy as I pass him and I'm sure his scowl deepens, which makes me giggle, and head for the stairs. Edward and Joe are waiting in the hallway, and I do a double take at how handsome Edward is. He's wearing navy chinos with a white shirt, and I groan inwardly because it occurs to me that we're matching. When he sees me, he grins.

'What are we, twins?' he asks, and I laugh.

'I can go and change.' I pause on the stairs.

'No, it's fine. Joe won't mind, will you?'

Joe looks from Edward to me and back again. 'Same colours,' he says. 'Matching.'

'That's right.' Edward scoops him up and swings him over his shoulder, making Joe screech with laughter. 'OK, then, do we have everything?'

I nod as I pick up the bag I left in the hallway earlier. It has a change of clothes for Joe as well as a birthday card that Polly procured from a cupboard in the kitchen. Apparently, she has a stock of cards for occasions like this.

'I've got the gift.' Edward goes to the hall table where a large box sits wrapped in brightly coloured paper. He tucks it under his free arm.

'That's very organised of you,' I say, impressed, although why wouldn't he be? I don't know him well enough to assume anything.

'My PA popped out during her lunchtime yesterday and got it. It's some sort of Lego rocket that's all the rage with the kids these days.' He raises his eyebrows as if he's baffled. 'I always thought Lego was great but had no idea it was so fashionable now.'

'That's because you're old, Daddy.' Joe giggles. He is still hanging over Edward's shoulder, his fair hair fanning out like a brush.

'Don't be cheeky, Joe, or I'll have to tickle you.'

'No, Daddy!' Joe wriggles and Edwards laughs.

'OK, maybe not now but later.' He looks at me. 'Ready?'

I nod then follow him out to the car where Jeff is waiting.

The journey to the grand Missenden Abbey takes twenty minutes and all the way there, Joe chats away like his life depends upon it. He's clearly excited about the party and seeing his friends. I'm content to listen while Edward responds to his son and occasionally asks him questions. Their relationship is sweet. Edward is a good father and in spite of everything he's been through, he still shows patience and understanding, still makes his young son feel valued. Not all people have that capacity for interacting with young children. I suspect that Edward might have wanted more children with his wife. Would they have had just one more or kept going? She was a model so perhaps she wouldn't have wanted to ruin her figure with multiple pregnancies. Or perhaps she didn't care and loved being pregnant and a mum. How sad then to be torn away from her husband and child before they had a chance to extend their family and before she could see Joe grow up. My heart hurts for the poor woman who lost out on so much. The more time I spend with Joe, the more I've started to think that one day, I'd like to have a family of my own, but with my vow to avoid men and love, it's unlikely to happen. Still, not everyone has to get married and have children. For some people, there are other priorities and mine are caring for my mum and brother. They need me and I'll always be there for them. I can't afford to let anyone else into my life if it means putting their welfare to one side.

Jeff stops the car right in front of the abbey and we get out. I reach for the bag with Joe's change of clothes but Edward stops me. 'Don't worry about it. Jeff won't go far.'

'Oh... OK.'

'Don't look like that.' Edward smiles. 'He'll go and get some refreshments and spend time with the other drivers. He's not expected to wait in the carpark all alone with nothing to eat or drink.'

'I'll just grab the card though.' I get the card from the bag then tuck it into my handbag.

Jeff gets back in the car and drives off around the side of the building.

'Ready Joe?' Edward asks.

'Ready, Daddy!' Joe takes Edward's hand then holds out his other hand to me. 'Come on, Ava.'

When I take his hand in mine, emotion wells inside me. I expected to walk with them but not be part of this human chain, Joe holding on to me like I'm part of their family. It's nice and I'm happy to join in. I can almost pretend that we are a little family unit of three.

Around the back of the abbey are grounds that stretch out for as far as the eye can see. There are trees to the left and right and dotted ahead on the landscape of endless green. Gazebos have been set up on the lawns and they appear to have different activities in each one which makes me think of the stalls at a fairground. And there are lots of people. This isn't a small birthday party like the ones Daniel has been to over the years. There are twenty children maximum at those parties but here, there are too many to count. There are also lots of adults, many of whom are very smartly dressed, some look like they've come expecting a day at the races. I suddenly feel self-conscious in my understated outfit. Perhaps I should have worn a dress. But then again, I am here to work.

We put the gift Edward's PA bought on the table that's groaning with other elaborately wrapped gifts and I add the card from my handbag, then we walk towards the gazebos.

Off to the left, I see that they actually have fairground rides. There's a mini Ferris wheel, a carousel, a house of mirrors and a helter skelter slide. It must have cost a fortune to hire the abbey and the rides, and all for a child's fifth birthday party.

Joe squeals with delight. 'Can I go on them all, Daddy?'
'We'll see.'
'Come on them with me, Daddy?' Joe tugs at Edward's hand. 'And you, Ava, come and have fun.'
Edward looks at me and raises his eyebrows in question.
'I'm game,' I say.
'Excellent.' Edward's eyes linger on my face for a moment as if he's trying to work something out, then he leads us towards the rides. We haven't even said hello to the birthday boy or his family yet and we're heading towards the fairground with all the enthusiasm and abandon of four-year-old Joe.

I giggle all the way, caught up on a wave of joy and excitement and it feels pretty good indeed.

Chapter 18

Edward

I honestly can't remember the last time I had this much fun. We arrived at the party and should have gone to see the Fitzroys first but instead, we went to the rides and I'm so glad we did. I knew Joe had energy but Ava really surprised me. Of course, she is younger than me by almost ten years but even so, she was enthusiastic about all the rides and even went down the helter skelter with Joe five times.

She's taken Joe to get a drink and I'm waiting for them when a hand touches my elbow.

'Hello, Edward.'

Turning, I find Hattie Fitzroy at my side.

'Hattie!' We kiss cheeks then she places her hands on my arms and leans back as she looks at me.

'You look good, darling.'

'Thanks.' I smile but she's shaking her head.

'We haven't seen you in far too long.'

'I know.' I look away for a moment, hoping we're not going to go *there*. 'I'm sorry.'

'No. Don't you be sorry. You've been to hell and back the past few years.'

Hattie and Lucille were friendly and through our wives, Tony and I became friendly too. Not great mates or anything, but we got on well enough when the four of us socialised together. Tony owns a luxury architectural design company which is how we've worked together. Hattie is pleasant enough, occasionally a bit overbearing, but she's a horse breeder and she's used to negotiating deals with all sorts of people so she's accustomed to speaking her mind and not taking any bullshit.

'Well... it was rough there for a while.'

Hattie nods, her blond bob shining in the late September sunshine. 'And how are you now?'

'Surviving.' These questions are always tough. What am I meant to say? I lost my wife in more ways than one? I was filled with self-loathing for quite some time? Self-loathing that hasn't entirely left me? I wish I could turn back the clock and... *And what? What would I do differently? Not be such a naive fucking bastard is what.*

'What is it?' Hattie touches my arm.

'Sorry?'

'Your face then... it was like a cloud passed over the sun.' She knits her brows. 'Are you sure you're all right?'

'I'm fine.' It's hard not to clench my jaw when people ask me questions like this and I long for the joy of simply being with Joe and Ava again. The joy of being able to forget for a while.

'Where's Joe?' Hattie looks around.

'Gone to get a drink.' I gesture at where Joe is standing with Ava while she adjusts the straw in his cup.

'Who's that he's with?' Hattie raises her fair brows and her lips curl upwards.

'That's Ava,' I say, not offering an explanation because I don't trust myself to speak yet.

'Well, isn't she just...' Hattie tilts her head as she stares at Ava. I shift from one foot to the other, wishing she wouldn't scrutinise Ava like that. 'Quite... petite. But curvy. Not at all like Lucille with her endless legs and flawless beauty.'

She turns back to me and scans my face and I feel a spark of anger in my gut. Who the hell is she to judge Ava for being who she is? Just because Hattie is wearing a designer dress and wedges doesn't mean Ava needs to do the same. But as I look at Ava now, I can see how plain her outfit is, how she would appear to someone like Hattie.

'It's nice that she dressed casually for today. Especially with all that sliding down the helter skelter.' So she saw that then? Saw Ava with me. Was she judging us?

'Ava's the nanny,' I say now, but it's not that I mean to explain that she's not *with* me, more that I want Hattie to understand why Ava is dressed that way and not more flamboyantly.

'Of course she is.' Hattie gives a relieved laugh. 'I can see it now.'

'Cynthia will be back after her holiday. Ava is covering for her while she's away and Joe really likes her.' After today and the fun we've had, so do I, but I don't add this. Banging on about how much I like the nanny will not go down well with Hattie, a woman who once adored my wife. A woman who sees the divide between classes as clearly as a brick wall.

'Well you have fun with her but don't hurt her, will you?' Hattie winks at me and I want to growl with fury.

'It's not like that!' I snap and Hattie looks at me as if I've grown another head.

'I'm sure it's not, darling.'

'Where's Charlie?' I ask, looking around although I can't see much other than the red mist in front of my eyes.

'Having some photographs done for one of the mags.'

I know what she means because Hattie loves a photoshoot and an Instagram grid, just like Lucille did. But selling your son's birthday party... It's not something I'd be happy doing. Lucille sold her pregnancy photos to a mag and after the accident I saw them everywhere. I couldn't escape from my pain and I don't want that for Joe. Ever.

'It paid for all this so what's a girl to do?' For some strange reason, Hattie does a small curtsey and I marvel at the fact that she's the way she is. I don't think I noticed when Lucille was around because they got on so well, kind of like a double act, and so her ways didn't grate on me in the way they are today. Perhaps it was her mentioning Lucille that got my back up or perhaps it's how dismissive she's being about Ava, but she's irritating the hell out of me and I can't wait to get away from her.

Ava and Joe are heading straight for us and I want to do something to stop them, to semaphore wildly that they should turn around and go back the way they came. I don't want Hattie speaking to Ava and hurting her. I'm fairly certain that's what she'll try to do, even if not deliberately, and I want to prevent that from happening but suddenly, it's too late.

'Hi.' Ava smiles at me then looks at Hattie.

'Hattie Fitzroy.' Hattie holds out a hand and Ava shakes it.

'Ava Thorne.'

'Aren't you a sweet little one?' Hattie chuckles. 'A rose without a thorn, right, Edward?'

Ava's eyes fill with confusion.

'Just so you know, Ava, if you need a new position after Cynthia returns, please give me a call. We can always do with an extra pair of hands to help out. Especially now.' She places a hand on her belly and I notice the curve of her stomach that I'd missed under the pattern of her brightly coloured dress.

'Congratulations.' I offer the words although part of me groans at the thought of her having another child. More Fitzroys to look down on the working class.

'Uhh... thanks,' Ava says finally. 'And congratulations.'

'Ta!' Hattie pats her belly. 'Think it's a girl. Hope it is. Don't want another bloody boy.' She chortles, and again, I see that Ava isn't sure how to react. 'Do you know, for a moment there I thought you were *with* Edward but then he told me that you're *just* the nanny. Such an amusing mistake for me to make! *LOL!* Anyway, I need to find my son so we can light the candles on the cake. Cheerio!'

She trots away on her wedges and an awkward silence falls between us. Joe is focused on his straw, but Ava looks mortified. I have an urge to pull her against my chest and hold her tight, to soothe away the dismay she feels at being called *just* the nanny. It's rude and unfair because no one is ever *just* something. Especially not Ava. This woman is warm, funny, kind and caring. She takes good care of my son. We've had fun together today.

I want us to have more fun together.

I want to see her smile again.

'Let's go and sing *Happy Birthday* then we can get going.' I gesture in the direction that Hattie went.

Ava nods but her eyes are filled with something I can't work out. I've never had someone call me *just* something, but I do know how it feels when you're not the person someone wants you to be. When you try to be what someone wants but you're you and you can't change that. I'm a successful businessman. I was also born into money and luxury. I want for nothing in financial terms. But that doesn't make me a heartless prick and I never set out to deliberately hurt anyone.

'Hey...' I place a hand on Ava's shoulder and she looks up at me. 'It's OK. Don't let Hattie get to you. I don't know about you, but I fancy a cold glass of wine when we get home and perhaps we could have a chat?'

She gives a small nod but it's like something has been lost and I'm filled with a sudden fear that we won't be able to get it back.

Chapter 19

Ava

When we arrive back at the house, I take Joe up to get him bathed and to bed. He fell asleep in the car and I watched as his eyelashes fluttered on his cheeks, wondering if he was dreaming about the fun he'd had that afternoon. I enjoyed myself too, was having a great time until my encounter with Hattie. I've met people like her before and, I guess, working for a billionaire businessman, there was always a chance it would happen again but despite my resolve to not allow her to hurt me, she did. People like that have the ability to look down their noses at others and it's horrible. I do try to value myself, perhaps not enough but I'm learning to do what I can, and yet a woman like that comes along and dismisses me as *just* the nanny.

It's people like me taking care of their children, cleaning their houses, washing their underwear and driving their cars that keep their worlds ticking over. A bit more respect would be nice. But I can't class them all as being the same. Edward has never shown me that kind of disrespect. He treats me and all of his staff with courtesy and yet... being there today and being treated that way by Harriet was a stark reminder that we come from very different worlds. Edward moves in circles I could never be a part of and Hattie made that very clear to me today.

When Joe is dressed in clean pyjamas, I get him to brush his teeth then tuck him into bed.

'Read me a story?' he asks.

I feel bone weary and just want to shower and go to sleep, but I do love story time with him and would never desert him before he's ready to drop off. Edward mentioned something earlier about cold, white wine but I'm not in the mood to drink and pretend everything is OK. However he sees me, I'm the hired help and that's all I'll ever be to him and his friends.

Joe chooses his story then I sit next to him on his bed.

'Ava?' he says, looking up at me.

'Yes, Joe.'

'I had fun today.'

'So did I, sweetheart.'

'Charlie has a mummy.'

I try to hide my shock at his words. I didn't see this coming.

'He does.' I don't say *and she's horrible* even though the words are on the tip of my tongue.

'I used to have a mummy.'

My throat closes over. 'Yes.' Nodding, I slide my arm around his shoulders.

'She's in heaven now. Daddy said she still loves us.'

'Of course she does.' I bite the inside of my cheek to stay in control. *Poor baby.*

'You won't go to heaven, will you?' His eyes are so earnest as he peers up at me that I have to bite harder on my cheek. 'I'd miss you.'

'I won't go to heaven. Not for a long time.'

He taps the book. 'You can read now.'

And just like that, the conversation is over and he has moved on. But it's a reminder that he thinks about these things and needs to feel secure.

When I start to read, he joins in with the bits he knows, and soon I feel him relax against me, his head resting against my arm. Peering down at him, I see that his eyes have closed. I close the book quietly then set in on the nightstand and slide him down so his head rests on the pillow.

I gently tuck the covers around him then sit back down again to wait for ten minutes in case he stirs. His blond hair is soft and shiny from the baby shampoo I used to wash it and his skin glows with health and vitality. He is four, almost five, in that stage between toddler and child. His wrists have lost the baby chubbiness but his cheeks still carry some of it and I can see how he would have looked as a baby. He is the sweetest child and we grow closer every day. I am, in fact, becoming worried that I'm growing too fond of him. Five weeks is a long time in the life of a child and he's already accepted me. I am the person he searches for in the morning, the one he calls for at night if he's had a bad dream. My contract states that I will be here until January rolls in, and I worry that in that time, we will be too attached. And yet, what can I do? I can hardly hold back from him, retain a professional air. He's four and he needs people around who'll love and nurture him.

With these thoughts swirling around my brain, I lean against the headboard and close my eyes. They are burning now with exhaustion so closing them offers me significant relief. A blissful warmth envelops me and I enjoy the sensation of floating as I drift away.

Chapter 20

Edward

The open bottle of Pinot Gris sits on the kitchen table, beads of condensation forming on the glass. I showered when we got in and put on some jersey shorts and an old T-shirt. Apart from Hattie's nonsense, we had a good day and I feel sad that she tainted it for Ava and for me. Ava didn't deserve that at all and I'm keen to try to repair the damage. I was hoping that some wine and perhaps a movie of her choice would make up for what happened at the party, but Ava took Joe to bed an hour ago and hasn't resurfaced. I was going to go in and say goodnight, but I could hear her reading him a story and I didn't want to disturb them. But now, I'd better go and check that he's not making her read twenty stories because he's quite good at manipulating people who care about him. I've fallen victim to *just one more story, Daddy, please* more than once.

Upstairs, I stop in the doorway of Joe's bedroom. The sight before me takes my breath away.

Joe is tucked into bed and Ava is next to him. They are both fast asleep. Ava is curled up on her side facing Joe and he's mirroring her as if they fell asleep whispering to each other. Ava's hair has come out of its ponytail, and it tumbles down over the pillow. In sleep, all self-consciousness has fallen away from her face, her dark lashes flutter on her cheeks and she is utterly beautiful.

Something inside me shifts and it makes me grip the doorframe.

What the hell is happening to me?

I barely know this woman and yet, what I do know of her, I like. We had fun today. She made me laugh. Not just surface laughter but deep belly laughs. The heaviness I've carried around with me slipped away as we went from ride to ride, as I watched her with my son, caring for him, nurturing him in the way a mother would do. Ava isn't just professional with Joe, she's like Cynthia is with him. She genuinely cares and that's all I can ask for in the person who looks after my child.

I'm torn between wishing that I could spend the evening with Ava and not wanting to disturb her, but she looks so tranquil that it seems unfair to wake her now. So I take the soft blanket from Joe's chair and gently place it over Ava, tuck it around her shoulders. This close, I can smell her perfume, some light apple scent that mingles with her coconut conditioner. It makes me imagine burying my face in her hair and breathing her in, holding her against me in the way I've imagined doing recently. She shifts slightly and I step back, not wanting to startle her if she wakes and finds me gazing at her like some kind of weirdo.

Am I a weirdo staring at the sleeping nanny like this? It could be seen that way but there's something going on here and it's confusing the hell out of me. Ava is... getting to me.

Dragging myself away is hard but I can't overstep the line. I stand in the doorway for a moment, taking a mental snapshot of my son and Ava, wanting to capture the peacefulness of the scene, and then I turn off the light and leave them in peace.

As I pad down the stairs to the kitchen and pour myself a large glass of wine, I know that I need to do something nice for Ava. But what? And then it occurs to me that it's her birthday next week.

I know exactly what I'm going to do to show her how valued she is, how much we appreciate her and everything she's done already. And then, perhaps, I can broach the subject of a different kind of contract because it's becoming clear to me that Ava could be the perfect fake wife.

Chapter 21

Ava

On the morning of my birthday, I wake and open the curtains to find a bright October morning. Autumn is definitely in the air now and I take a moment to enjoy the view from my bedroom window. As much as I miss Mum and Daniel, I don't miss the view of the small green in front of the flat with its sparse patch of grass and the flats opposite. There are always teenagers hanging around outside in the afternoons and while I know it's not their fault — after all, they have nowhere else to go — it can be intimidating for some people to walk past them.

My phone is on the bedside table so I grab it then swipe the screen and see a message from Mum. She's sent me a photo of a banner hung in the kitchen with *Happy Birthday!* on it. Daniel is standing underneath, already in his school uniform. My heart squeezes because I always spend my birthdays with them and here I am, turning twenty-six and they're not with me. I reply to Mum telling her that I love them then head to the bathroom to brush my teeth and jump in the shower before waking Joe up for school.

When I get to Joe's room, he's not there. His bed is

made and his curtains open. My stomach lurches with anxiety because on the rare occasions that he's woken up early, he always waits for me to take him downstairs now. It's become part of the routine he enjoys. Some days, he'll be in bed still sleeping, others he'll be in bed reading and a few times I've found him on the floor playing with some of his toys. For such a young child, he's incredibly well behaved, and I often think about what life has been like for him with his father grieving and his mother gone. All children deserve to have their parents around for them but I know that's not always the reality. Look at me and Daniel, for example. Our father has been gone a long time, returning for brief visits when he'd pretend to care before disappearing again. He doesn't care if we're alive or dead and I often feel that way about him. He abandoned his family to chase a dream and I'll never understand how he could do that.

I leave the room and head downstairs, thinking that Joe will probably be in the kitchen with Polly, but when I get there, the kitchen door is closed. Polly always leaves the door open because Edward, Joe and I wander in and out all the time. Not wanting to intrude if she's closed it for a reason, I knock and wait. When it swings inwards, I jump as I'm greeted with, 'Happy Birthday, Ava!'

Standing around the table are Edward, Joe, Polly and Jeff and on the table are several neatly wrapped gifts, an enormous bouquet of sunflowers and a pile of envelopes.

'Joe runs to me and hugs my legs then says, 'Open your presents, Ava, and see what I chose for you.'

He leads me to the table and I sit down then he climbs up next to me.

'Breakfast won't be long, dear,' Polly says, laying a hand on my shoulder. I am overcome by emotion because I really didn't expect this. I thought today would be a quiet affair, that I'd get Joe ready for school then spend the day as I usually do, perhaps speaking to Mum and Daniel for a bit longer this afternoon. But it seems that I've been spoilt, and I don't know how to react.

'Thank you all so much,' I say.

Edward smiles at me and my stomach fills with butterflies. Since the day out at Charlie's party a week ago, things have felt a bit strange between us, like there's something unfinished in the air. That night, I didn't make it downstairs to share some wine with him because I fell asleep next to Joe. I woke in the early hours to find that someone, presumably Edward, had tucked a blanket around me. The thought that he'd done something so caring warmed me right through. I folded the blanket, tucked Joe in then went to my own room and got straight into bed without brushing my teeth because I was so exhausted. The next day, Edward took Joe out to visit one of his friends, so I didn't see either of them until late afternoon. It meant that Edward and I didn't talk about what had happened at the party and as the days passed, I didn't feel I should raise it. Perhaps he'd thought nothing of it after all and I was imagining that he cared. But now he's done this on my birthday and I'm even more confused.

'Here you go.' Joe hands me a small gift as reverently as if he's handing me the crown jewels. 'You're going to like this, Ava.'

'Don't tell her what it is, Joe!' Edward warns.

'Hurry up!' Joe bounces on his seat so I do my best to get the paper off.

Inside is a small blue box so I remove the lid.

'It's because you like reading,' Joe says, a grin spreading from ear to ear. 'I chose it, didn't I, Daddy!'

Meeting the Billionaire Boss

'He did.' Edward nods.

'Put it on!' Joe is very bossy this morning, but I know it's because he's excited.

Carefully, I take the silver chain from the box and admire the small silver book that I realise is a locket.

'You can put a photo inside it.' Joe taps the locket. 'Of me if you want.'

'It's beautiful.' I fasten the chain around my neck and touch the locket where it rests against my skin, smiling at the thought of him wanting his photo there.

'Now open the others,' Joe says, pointing at the rest of the gifts.

There's a pretty jade scarf and matching gloves from Polly (for the colder weather), a book from Jeff (the latest thriller everyone's talking about, apparently, he tells me), a few more gifts from Joe and Edward (including some fancy-looking Belgian chocolates and a pair of navy wellies with bright yellow bees all over them), the enormous bouquet of sunflowers and then the cards. I open them all and find one from Mum and Daniel and my heart aches, wishing they were here too.

'Right, clear that lot to the other end of the table,' Polly says and she bustles around the kitchen before placing a huge plate of chocolate chip pancakes in the middle followed by a large bowl of fruit salad and a plate of crispy bacon. My mouth waters at the incredible smell.

Edward fills glasses with freshly squeezed orange juice and Polly adds a pot of coffee to the feast.

'Dig in!' she says, winking at me.

The kitchen falls quiet as we eat and I gaze at the people around the table, aware that I'm growing fond of them all. It's dangerous to care about people you work with and for, but I can't help it. All they've shown me is kindness and acceptance and today they've proven that they're genuinely nice people. My birthday was something I thought would pass by unnoticed but somehow, because I didn't tell them, they knew it was today, and they've made an effort to spoil me. At this rate, I'm never going to want to leave.

Once breakfast is done and the plates cleared away, I get up and thank them all again. 'Come on then, Joe, we'd better get your things ready to go.'

'I want to stay home with you.' He pouts and folds his arms across his chest.

'It's Friday so we can spend tomorrow together instead,' I reply, hoping that he'll be OK with that. I'd love to spend the day playing with him and giving my new wellies a trial walkabout, but he has school and routines are important.

'Go on, Joe. Get your bag and shoes,' Edward says, and Joe nods resignedly then leaves the table.

'I have something planned for this evening,' Edward says once Polly is busy at the sink and Jeff has gone to bring the car around to take Joe to school.

'No problem. I can see to Joe,' I say, smiling. 'Thanks again for all this.' I gesture at the kitchen.

'No... I mean... I have something planned for *you* for this evening.'

'Oh... OK.'

'If you can be ready for six, that would be great. And uh... I've got something for you to wear.' He worries his bottom lip. 'I don't want to overstep the mark but where we're going, you'll need something a bit special.'

Now I really am lost for words. *Where we're going? A bit special?*

I cough to clear my throat and mumble, 'OK, thanks.' Then I nod before slipping from the room because I am blushing like a schoolgirl who's just been asked on her first date.

But then something occurs to me... Oh god, he's not taking me to meet some of his posh friends is he? Or to something like a sex dungeon where I'll find out that he's a secret Dom or something. Did I miss something in the employment contract about having to accompany him to a *certain kind* of club? Is that why he's got me something 'a bit special' to wear? Is it black leather with appendages?

Don't be ridiculous, Ava! He's not like that at all.

You never know what someone's like until you know them well, is something my mother always told me. And she was right. She thought she knew my dad until he buggered off with his band dreaming of making millions when he found fame and fortune. For all I know or care he's still searching. Mum also says, you never know what someone's like until you need them, and that applied to my dad too. *Utter bastard!*

Anxiety prickles on my skin because I'm not good at surprises and I have no idea what Edward has planned for me. But I'm sure it can't be anything bad because he's been nothing but kind so far. Well, apart from when he caught me watching his wedding DVD and I shouldn't have done that anyway, so...

We will see. And now I have to wait until this evening before I'll know what my surprise is. Perhaps I should read 'Fifty Shades...' again to prepare.

It's going to be a long old day.

Chapter 22

Ava

By the time 5.45pm comes, my head is whirling. Not only did Edward send me a box containing a beautiful dress, a pair of sleek heels and a bag — not a leather garment in sight, thank goodness — but he also brought in a hairstylist and makeup artist. The two women are polite and friendly, but also very professional, and they tend to me as if I'm royalty not an agency childcare worker. It's odd and I feel out of place, embarrassed and awkward, and yet I tell myself to accept their ministrations because this is what Edward has asked me to do. It would be rude to turn away from this pampering, surely? Even if it is certainly not something I'm used to. Back when I reached the end of my time at school at sixteen, most of the other girls were obsessed with prom from what they were wearing, to having their hair and nails done and spray tans, but I didn't allow myself to care about it at all. Why not? I knew I couldn't go to prom. How could we have afforded a dress and all the other expenses that seemed to go along with it? That afternoon, I peered out of the window as other girls who lived nearby went out to the cars that were taking them to the hotel booked for the occasion. I felt like Cinderella being left behind when her stepsisters go to the ball. After the cars had disappeared into the distance, I went and cuddled up to Mum on the sofa and watched TV. She didn't even know that it was prom that night and I'd never have said anything because I didn't want her to worry. So today, this is extra special, and it is Edward that I must thank for it.

When I am left alone, I take a few minutes to steady myself. Looking into the full-length mirror, I can barely believe this is me. I look like a model or celebrity going to an awards event. Admittedly, I don't wear makeup normally, but I do like the gentle transformation. The silver and grey shadows that the makeup artist used have made my amber eyes seem darker, seem — if I dare admit it — sultry. My hair has been curled and piled on top of my head with my fringe swept to one side and a few curled tendrils have been left down around the sides of my face and my neck. The makeup artist also did my nails and while I didn't want her to stick on fake ones, as I'm not used to having long nails, she did paint them a lovely dark purple to match the dress.

As for the dress, it's not something I'd have picked for myself — not that I could ever have afforded to buy it — because it's very fitted and clings to my curves. But somehow, it doesn't make me look like I'm heavy, instead it fits like it was made for me. I like how I look in it and wonder if that's because it was probably so expensive. The purple satin heels are high, something else I'm not used to, but they're very pretty and I walk up and down a few times to get used to how they feel. I hope I don't fall over and embarrass us both!

And so, when I feel ready, I leave my room and walk to the landing. I swear I hear Mr Darcy wolf-whistle at me, so I flash him a smile then take a deep breath before descending.

Chapter 23

Edward

I'm talking to Joe in the hallway about how he must be good for Polly this evening when I look up and see her. It's like I've been sucker-punched because my breath leaves my body in a whoosh and I have to shake my head and look again.

'Goodness me, Ava, don't you look incredible!' Polly snaps me out of my spell and I go to the bottom of the stairs and hold out a hand.

Ava takes my hand and steps off the last stair. She's trembling slightly and I realise that she might not be used to wearing such high heels, so I slide my arm around her waist and smile at her, wanting her to know she's safe and can relax. But fuck, when I touch her, when I feel her warmth against me and smell her delicious fragrance, my whole body stirs.

'You do look incredible,' I say to her, hoping she knows exactly how gorgeous she is.

'I don't feel I look like me.' She nibbles at her bottom lip and I shake my head.

'You do look like you. Just a version of you that's been pampered. You're beautiful.'

'Thank you,' she replies but I can see the uncertainty in her eyes. Hopefully an evening of fun will help with that.

'I want to come,' Joe says, folding his arms across his small chest and scowling at us.

'Not this evening. We're going somewhere for grownups. But we'll do something together over the weekend.'

'Promise, Daddy?'

'I promise.'

'Ava looks like a princess,' he says. *That's my boy!*

'We'd better get going then,' I say. 'Oh... wait a moment. There's something in my pocket.'

I reach into my jacket pocket and pull out a box then hold it out for Ava.

'What is it?' she asks.

I release her and open the box so she can see.

'For me?' she asks.

'For you.' I nod. 'Can I help you put it on?'

'Please.' She turns and I fasten the necklace around her slim neck. My instinct is to press a kiss to her nape above the clasp, but for many obvious reasons, I don't. I haven't been intimate with a woman for a long time and being around Ava, especially when she looks and smells this good, is playing havoc with me.

When she turns back to face me, I smile. 'It's perfect.'

The Tiffany platinum pendant holds a pear-shaped tanzanite surrounded by sparkling diamonds. The violet-blue of the tanzanite matches the dress perfectly. It sits just above the locket from Joe and both draw attention to Ava's milky-white decolletage and the swell of her full breasts cradled by the bodice of the dress. She looks good enough to eat and I reprimand myself inwardly. I'm not supposed to be ogling my employee. Not at all. Tonight is about treating her to a good time and then bringing her home safe, smiling and untouched.

'Thank you so much.' Ava places a hand over the pendant. 'It's gorgeous.'

I hold out my arm. 'Shall we go to the ball?'

'I'd like that.' She hooks her arm through mine, and we walk to the door.

'Don't stay up too late,' I say to Joe and Polly, offering Polly a conspiratorial wink. I told her that Joe could have an extra story before bed and she laughed. On occasion, when Cynthia was unavailable, Polly has helped out with Joe and I know that she, like all my employees, adores him.

'We'll have fun, won't we, Joe?' Polly says and my son grins up at her.

'With hot chocolates?'

'That's our secret!' Polly fakes a horrified look and I laugh.

'See you later.' I wave at them then escort Ava to the car, and I find that I'm looking forward to the evening more than I've looked forward to anything in a very long time.

Chapter 24

Ava

When we reach London, and Jeff drives through the busy streets, my stomach flutters with anticipation. I have no idea where we're going and it's exciting to have someone take control, someone who cares enough to want to surprise me.

'How're you feeling?' Edward asks.

'Excited,' I reply, then I admit, 'I never went to prom so getting dressed up like this and being chauffeur driven is all new to me.'

'What? That's awful!' He frowns.

'It's OK. This is even better.' And it is. I'm having a wonderful time already.

'Good. It's not far.' He turns his body towards me. 'Ava... can you trust me?'

'What do you mean?'

'Well... I really would like where we're going to be a surprise so... Could you wear this?'

I look down and see that he's holding a blindfold. It's a black silk one, the kind you wear for sleeping.

'You want to blindfold me?'

For some reason the thought sends a thrill shooting through me. Edward is asking to be completely in control. I have never allowed a man to dominate me in any way because that would mean handing over my trust and after what my father did, I've been opposed to trusting men. But Edward has given me no reason *not* to trust him. I find that I want to put my faith in him. He's done all this for me, bought me this beautiful dress, shoes and necklace. He's shown that he's thoughtful, kind and caring. So somehow, deep down, I find the courage to put my faith in him and I know that it'll be OK. It does cross my mind that this could be because we're going to the type of club I thought about previously, but I decide to wait and see.

'Not for long, I promise.' He smiles, sealing the deal for me, so I take the blindfold and slip it on, taking care to keep it loose at the front so it doesn't ruin my eye makeup.

My other senses now take over and I feel the motion as Jeff stops the car and opens the back door. There is a rush of air as Edward gets out then he takes my hand and helps me out too. Every time I take his hand, I get a jolt of electricity up my arm that leaves me breathless. It's ridiculous really, feeling this way at just the touch of a man's hand. But then it's been a long time since a man held my hand. A long time since a man touched me anywhere. How would it feel if Edward touched me in other places? If he ran his fingers over my breasts or slid a hand up my thigh... That's a thought I push away because it's never going to happen, even if right now I wish it would.

I hear Jeff start the engine and drive away then Edward asks, 'You OK?' He is close to me, his breath tickling the skin of my cheek, my neck, waving the tendrils of hair near my ear.

'I'm OK.' My voice wavers so I clear my throat.

He slides my hand through his arm and I'm pulled closer to him. There's the swish of a sliding door and the cool of an air-conditioned lobby, the click of my heels on shiny tiles.

'Good evening, Mr Cavendish.' A deep voice from our left.

'Good evening, Blake.' Edward leans closer to me. 'A security guard I know. We're going to the lifts now, Ava.'

With him guiding me, I walk as confidently as I can in the heels and without being able to see. There's another swish and then we step forwards and Edward turns me then takes my hands and places them on two walls either side of me. I'm guessing that I'm facing out into the lift but I can't be sure.

'I'm going to remove the blindfold now,' he says and I feel him move closer. I can sense him standing very close to me and my whole body tingles. If he was to touch me now, to brush his hands over my breasts, would I try to stop him? Somehow, I don't think so.

My imagination is running away with me and so, when he gently touches the sides of my head where the blindfold sits and lifts it away, I experience a flicker of disappointment. The fantasy of having Edward touch me all over while I am blindfolded is one I will have to store away for a different time when I am alone.

I blink at the brightness while my eyes adjust.

'Where are we?' I ask, looking around. Our reflections dance around us in the mirrored walls, and above us on the ceiling, images flash. A screen high on the wall shows an outline of a building and then I realise where we are. 'The Shard?'

'Yes.' His eyes search my face. 'Have you been here before?'

I snort. 'No. I couldn't afford to come to a place like this.'

'It's not that expensive, surely? I mean, for a trip in the lift along with a drink and a bite to eat?'

'Not for a billionaire, no.' His face falls and I shake my head. 'I'm sorry. I didn't mean to snap. It's just that... we didn't have anything spare for days out and... and things like this.'

'Were things that tight for you?' A tiny line has appeared between his brows and I want to smooth it away. I don't want to be the cause of his frowns.

'I thought you looked into my background.'

'I did. But not forensically. My guy... he checked that you didn't have a criminal record, social media accounts or a best friend who's a journalist and yes, I knew that your finances weren't in great shape but—' He meets my eyes. 'I'm sorry. I know that sounds bad but see... I needed to be sure about you. Joe needs someone we can rely on to care for him, not one of those nannies who'll sell his baby photos to the papers, who'll make up stories about me and my family and post our private moments all over Instagram. I've seen it happen before to people I know and it's never pretty. Lives can be ruined. Businesses destroyed. So while I had an overview of your life, I didn't see the bare bones of it. I don't know what your childhood was like in any great detail or what you had for dinner every day.'

'Oh.' I exhale and feel myself sag slightly as my reality enters the lift space with us like the Ghost of Christmas Past.

I'm aware of what we look like together this evening. A wealthy couple dressed in their finest. Me in my designer dress and heels, a precious stone at my throat; him in his black suit with a crisp, white shirt open at the collar and his devastatingly handsome face. We look like we have money and a good life. We look like we belong together. But our realities are incredibly different. Edward has money and an affluent lifestyle. I have a life of struggle. Of worrying about where the next meal will come from. Of not knowing what tomorrow will bring if I screw up this opportunity.

But then it hits me.

Edward might have money but he has lost the woman he loves and no money can make up for that.

'Hey, what is it?' He gently takes my chin between his thumb and forefinger and raises it. 'Don't be sad on your birthday. Let me show you a good evening. Please. I know... of course I know... that money can make a lot of things in life easier, but it can't buy happiness. Not unless you share it.' He strokes my chin with his thumb and my nerve endings tingle. It would be so easy to kiss him now and to encourage him to slide his hand lower. The hard pulsing between my legs yearns for his touch and the relief it would bring.

But I do neither. Instead, I take some slow, deep breaths and try to calm my racing heart. Edward is right. We're here at The Shard. We have a pleasant evening ahead of us and I am not going to let anything ruin it. It's time to enjoy this birthday present and to look forward to a future that will be very different to the past.

The lift stops and the doors open then we step out onto the 52nd floor. Edward takes my hand and as we walk into the bar, I am struck dumb by the sheer elegance and beauty of the sight that lies before me.

Chapter 25

Ava

Darkness has fallen outside and the room glows with spotlighting above tables and the bar itself. Dark furniture adds to the atmosphere while foliage adorns some of the planters and fittings, making it seem like we are in a dense forest or woodland hideaway. There are sofas to our left and booths to the right alongside the window.

'It's so quiet here.' I glance at Edward and see his mouth twitch. 'Why is that?'

He shrugs but I nudge him. 'You didn't?'

'Of course not.' He laughs but I know in that moment that he has rented the bar just for us.

'But how?'

He turns to me and cocks an eyebrow. 'Really?'

'OK, I get it, money opens doors and buys whatever you want. But also, wow!' Not only has he brought me to an exclusive bar at The Shard but also rented it out for just the two of us. If I wasn't such a practical person, I might just swoon at the sheer romance of it all. If it was a romantic scenario, that is, because this isn't a date. It's a night out, a birthday celebration a boss is providing for his employee. But it's hard to hold on to those facts when we're dressed like this, when the few members of staff in the space are quiet and discrete, waiting to tend to our every whim.

'Where would you like to sit?' he asks and sweeps his arm around us.

'By the window of course!' Part of me wishes I could pull out my phone and take some photos to show Mum and Daniel but I don't for two reasons. One: Edward might think I was planning on posting them somewhere. Two: I don't want to do anything that takes me away from being right here, right now. No man has ever done anything like this for me before and I doubt any man ever will do again. Therefore, I'm going to treasure every second.

We go to a small round table and sit in two plush blue velvet tub chairs. It's a relief to sit down because the heels are already making my calves ache.

I lean forwards and take in the view. Ahead of us, London stretches out, a city of lights. Tower Bridge is right there, lit up, and the lights are reflected in the darkness of The Thames. 'It's incredible up here.'

'I hoped you'd think so.'

When I turn to him, Edward is gazing at me in a way that makes my stomach fizz and I haven't taken a sip of alcohol yet.

'Champagne or cocktails?' Edward asks.

'Surprise me.'

He raises one brow. 'I thought I'd already done that.'

'And you're doing brilliantly so far...' I tilt my head, surprising myself because I'm being flirtatious, but it seems to be coming naturally now and I'm convinced it's because of Edward. He brings out a version of me I've never met before.

A waiter appears at Edward's elbow and he whispers into the man's ear then we're left alone again.

'Did you ever want to come here?' he asks. 'I know you said you couldn't afford to but was it somewhere you'd have liked to visit? Or were there other places?'

I look down at my hands with their sparkly nails and moisturised cuticles. So different this evening from the wrinkled hands that spent so long sweating in rubber gloves scrubbing hotel baths, showers and toilets. 'There was no point wanting anything like that. Wanting only leads to dissatisfaction. I think I got to a point where I didn't dare to daydream.'

'God, Ava, that's so sad.'

Closing my eyes, I breathe in deeply, exhale slowly. 'I had people relying on me. I didn't have time to waste being self-indulgent. But, no... I'm not being completely honest. I read a lot to escape and, of course, that fuelled my dreams, but I was pretty good at putting them into a box in my mind and locking them away.'

'What dreams did you allow yourself?' His eyes are fixed on my face, filled with intense curiosity, and I feel like he can see down to the bottom of my soul.

My cheeks flood with heat and I turn my head away from him. I'm not sharing those dreams with anyone.

'Ava?' He's leaning towards me and when I do look at him, I see the mischief in his eyes. 'You don't have a... a boyfriend? Or partner?'

I shake my head. 'Not for a long time.'

'How long?'

'*Very* long.'

'What a waste.' His words are whispered but they make

the hairs on my arms rise and a flush of pleasure roars through me like a tidal wave.

And then the waiter returns with a tray of drinks and there's no need for me to respond but Edward's words linger with me like the sweetest kiss.

Chapter 26

Edward

Hearing that it's been a long time since Ava had a boyfriend pleases me more than it should. I know it shouldn't matter and yet it does. In a way, it makes it easier to consider the proposal I want to make to her. It also sends my sex-starved brain off in other directions where I know it shouldn't go.

How long since she's been kissed? Touched? Fucked?

I reach for the drinks that the waiter brought and hold one out to Ava.

'Here.'

'What is it?' she asks as she accepts the glass.

'It's a Don Juancho. It has rum, banana peel syrup, sherry, bitters and tonka beans.'

'I don't even know what some of those are,' she says laughing.

'Try it.' I raise my glass to her and watch as she takes a sip. Her eyes widen and delight broadens her smile.

'Yum! That's so good.'

'I know, right?'

We sip our drinks and gaze at the view, and I relax into

my chair. I like this bar, have been here several times, but never alone with a woman. Perhaps I've gone a bit overboard for Ava but I find that I want to impress her. I want her to have fun. I want to introduce her to the things she's never experienced because she deserves to enjoy herself. Perhaps it's the alpha businessman in me showing off as well, wanting to impress this beautiful young woman because every time she smiles, I feel like I'm winning. Perhaps it's something about her innocence that makes me want to show her things, a bit like taking her virginity and bringing her the joy of knowledge and experience.

When our glasses are empty, I point to the tray. There are more cocktails on there because I wanted Ava to try a variety.

'Go on then,' she says. Her cheeks are rosy and her eyes shining but I can see that she's relaxing so it's all good.

'Let's have this one next.' I hand her a glass. 'It's an Amazonia.'

I watch as she tastes it, licking her lips. 'Mmm. Kind of bitter-sweet.'

'It's got gin, mezcal and fortified wine.'

She giggles and I swear my cock stirs at the sound.

Two cocktails later, I can feel the gentle buzz of alcohol in my veins. We've been talking about my business because Ava asked what I do, but I suspect that she doesn't think it's that interesting. I mean, it's construction and not everyone cares about meeting with architects and councils, about creating energy efficient buildings, negotiating deals, land acquisition and all that comes with it. I tried to keep it simple but I know that sometimes I can get carried away and bore my audience. It's the construction geek in me.

'Edward,' she says, when I place my glass on the table.

'Yes?'

'I think I'm a bit tipsy. I was trying to focus on what you were saying but my head's a bit fuzzy.' She bites her bottom lip in a way that makes me instantly hard then takes my hand, which does nothing to ease my arousal. 'Sorry.'

'Don't be sorry.' I shift in my seat, trying to get comfy. 'We need some food to soak the cocktails up.'

'Definitely.' She nods.

I wave at the barman, and he gives me a thumbs up. Within no time at all, a delicious array of food is delivered to our table along with a bottle of champagne.

I fill our glasses then hand one to Ava and raise mine. 'Happy Birthday, Ava. I hope this next year will be wonderful for you.'

'Thank you so much, Edward.'

We clink glasses then drink. I notice that she's fidgeting a bit, so I ask, 'You OK?'

She leans towards me and whispers, 'It's these shoes. They're gorgeous but my feet aren't used to heels.'

'Hold on.' I get up and kneel down then take her feet on my lap. Gently, I undo the buckles and slide her dainty feet out of the heels. I place the shoes under the table then massage her feet for a moment where I can see that the shoes have dug in. However expensive shoes are, there's no guarantee that they won't cause discomfort. 'Better?'

I meet Ava's gaze and there's something in her eyes that makes me want to lift her feet and kiss them, to suck on her tiny toes and worship her in the way she should be worshipped. Fuck, this woman is doing things to me that could cause my downfall. My hand strays from her foot, slides slowly up to her knee and her eyes darken, her lips part. It would be so easy to keep going until I part her shapely thighs and move her lacy underwear aside. To stroke the most sensitive parts of her then follow the path of my fingers with my mouth. To taste her right here, right now then drink her as she comes against my tongue.

But I don't. I can't cross that line with her, especially not when she's tipsy and looking at me like that. I don't want to hurt her and ruin things for us and for Joe. And I know I would hurt her because my heart isn't how it used to be. I don't think I'll ever be able to love again.

Reluctantly, I slide my hand back down and gently place her feet on the floor then I sit back in my seat and drain my glass. When I look at Ava again, I'm glad I held back. The last thing I want is to take advantage of her in any way. Especially in light of the business proposition I have for her because fucking her now could really mess with her head.

And she's far too special for that.

Chapter 27

Ava

After we have eaten, Edward asks if I want to see the roof terrace. Giddy with everything that's happened this evening, I agree. He pours what's left of the champagne into our glasses and we go outside.

The view is spectacular. We stand at the protective glass barrier and gaze out at London. The perspective is dizzying and adds to my giddy feeling.

'This has been my best birthday ever,' I say.

'Really?'

'Yes.'

'You've had twenty-five birthdays before this one and not one of them has matched up to this?'

'Mum always does what she can but this is very different.' I glance at him. 'I've never been so pampered. It's like I've stepped into someone else's shoes. Someone else's life.'

'What if this could be your life?' he says.

'That's impossible.' I laugh. 'The money you're paying me will make a big difference, but it won't buy this.'

'No, I know. But you could have this life.' He places a hand on my shoulder and turns me gently. 'Ava, I... I have a proposition for you. It's a tough one to put to you but seeing you here this evening, you fit. You might not think you do but this lifestyle suits you.'

'I don't understand what you're saying.' I look at the glass in my hand. How much have I had to drink? Am I hallucinating now? Will Mr Darcy from the portrait pop up next to Edward any moment and I'll have two of them to deal with? If I drink much more, I probably will start seeing double.

'You're trembling,' he says, frowning. And I realise I am. It might be beautiful up here but it's October and I'm wearing a thin dress. He removes his jacket then wraps it around my shoulders. It carries his body heat and his scent, and I instinctively nestle into it, hold it in front of me with one hand. 'Better?'

'Yes.'

'So... my proposition. And there's no pressure at all to agree. It will not affect your current position or salary or how I see you. I have to clarify that first.'

'OK.' Now I'm really confused.

'Ava... to inherit what is rightfully mine, I have to meet a clause in my grandfather's will. The clause states that I need to be married on my thirty-fifth birthday.'

I scan his face. I don't understand what this has to do with me.

'Fuck this is so embarrassing.' He rubs at his brow.

'Wait a moment... so if you're not married, you lose your business?'

He nods. 'It's not mine yet because Grandpa only passed away seven months ago and he had no intention of handing anything over while he was still alive. He put a clause in his will that states I have to be married to a woman on and for a year after my thirty-fifth birthday in order to inherit his shares and be CEO. Following my birthday, the board will meet and vote on the next CEO and I want that to be me.'

'When is your birthday?'

'May.'

'That seems rather... archaic.'

He inclines his head. 'My grandpa was a stubborn old goat and when he got something into his head, there was no persuading him to change his mind. Not long before he died, he asked if I'd marry again and I told him no. The clause in his will was his response. I didn't find out that he'd changed his will until after he'd passed away. I think he wanted me to be married so I didn't end up alone like my father and also because it's good for appearances. Plus he clearly got cheesed off when I said I'd never marry again and this was him having revenge from beyond the grave. He liked people to bend to his will and I'm a bit stubborn too so I wouldn't have done something just to please him.'

'Can't you question the will now?'

'I could and it might get me his shares, but the board is made up of a lot of his friends and they'd vote against me becoming CEO out of loyalty to him.'

'What happens to the business if you lose it?'

'It'll be bought by some wealthy businessperson or sold off to other shareholders probably, possibly even sold to a competitor and closed down. The family name would likely go and the business I grew up wanting to be at the head of will no longer exist. This business is my life, Ava. It's all I ever wanted growing up.'

'What will you do?' I feel for him, I really do. It's such a difficult situation.

'I need to find a bride.'

'I'm sure there are plenty of willing women.' I sip my

drink, enjoying the crisp, clear taste even though I suspect I've had enough alcohol now. This all seems so surreal.

'That's the problem. See... I don't want to marry for love again. It's too painful if something goes wrong. I need a wife who understands our arrangement.'

'Arrangement?'

'It would be an arrangement with a contract... a prenup that would mean the woman would be protected. She'd also be financially stable for the rest of her life. We'd have to live together for a while after the wedding to convince people it was real...' He rubs at his neck.

Edward looks incredibly uncomfortable now. I feel like I'm trying to do a jigsaw but the pieces are floating around me and I can't quite put them together.

'Well... I hope you find someone.' Jealousy pierces my heart like a dagger. He's going to marry someone and then... And then, what? What did I expect to happen here? 'If I knew anyone suitable, I'd suggest them, but I don't.'

He rubs the back of his neck again then holds my gaze. 'Ava... What I'm trying to ask you is... How would you feel about... about marrying me?'

'Me?' The jigsaw pieces fall suddenly into place. My hand flies to my chest in shock and his jacket slips from my shoulders. He catches it as it falls and wraps it back around me.

'It would be a marriage without romance and love... but it would offer you other things. And you said you don't have a partner or boyfriend and you've been struggling financially but I'd make sure you wanted for nothing.'

I watch him carefully. 'You'd pay me to marry you?' This handsome, intelligent, ambitious man would pay me to be his bride?

'If you'll have me.'

He's serious. *Shit!* Or is he drunk too?

What he's suggesting would be a purely financial arrangement for me. I never thought I'd marry, have been dead set against becoming involved with anyone. But... is there a part of me that still believes in love? In marrying for love? Or could I marry for money and a better lifestyle? It wouldn't just be about me, of course, it would be about Mum and Daniel too. And... I'd be there for Joe as he grows up. If the marriage lasted that long.

'Let me check I heard you correctly? You're asking me to marry you? But not for love? This would be an arrangement that would be financial for me and involve an inheritance for you?'

'That's right.' He presses his lips together. 'Look. It's been a busy evening and it's your birthday and I don't want to put any pressure on you. Take some time to think about it. There's no rush. Well, not until next year. May, to be precise. You can take until the end of your nannying contract to decide if you like.' He drags his lower lip through his teeth.

'What is it?'

'Well, if you then decide not to marry me, I'll have to find someone else and I'll have even less time.'

'Oh...'

'It's fine.' He waves a hand. 'Let's park the idea for now and you take some time to think about it.'

'Right. Thanks.'

I feel suddenly sober, as if someone has poured a bucket of cold water over my head. I'm a pragmatic person and I know that this arrangement would be a positive thing for me in many ways. Hell, if Nala had suggested it to me a few weeks ago, I'd have been more open to it I think. But now that I've got to know Edward, things are somewhat more complicated.

Why?

Because I'd be agreeing to marry *Edward*. He's not some faceless man I've never met. He's kind and funny, attractive and attentive. Could I marry him and not fall for him? It sounds like that could be a recipe for disaster for me because even if my affection for him grew, I don't think he'd return my feelings.

And yet, if I decline him, am I throwing away the opportunity of a lifetime?

Chapter 28

Ava

True to his word, Edward lets me have time to think. Two weeks pass and we carry on as normal. I look after Joe, I see Edward around the house in the mornings if I'm up early enough and then in the evenings. We did spend time with Joe the day after my birthday and took him to a local animal sanctuary where he got to pet rabbits and feed ducks and donkeys, but it was a strange day. On the way home from The Shard, we talked about music and movies, avoiding any reference to the serious conversation we'd had on the terrace overlooking London and I ended up wondering if I'd imagined it all.

I still don't know what to do and it's not exactly the type of conversation you can have with just anyone. I can't phone Mum and say, 'Hey Mum, I'm considering marrying for money. What do you think?' I'm sure she'd be shocked and while she's never tried to control me, she'd need to express her concerns. Part of me craves that sensible conversation, her sage advice that will make me think twice about jumping in, and yet part of me wants to say *to hell with it all, I'm going to go for it.* After all, up to this point, what has life thrown into my lap other than hardship and worry?

Marrying Edward would solve all my current problems.

My main concern is whether it would present me with new ones.

It's half term and I have the day off because Edward is taking Joe out, so I've arranged to meet up with Nala. She got me this job in the first place so perhaps I can speak to her about what's on the table now. I don't have any close friends because I've been so busy working since I left college, and I've lost touch with the friends I had back then. With no social media, it's hard to stay in contact and in a way I was glad to let distance grow between us because my life was always very different from theirs.

I drive the car Edward has given me, albeit for a loan, to our lunch date and park it far away from other vehicles because I'm terrified someone will bump it or scratch it with their door. We're meeting at a rural 17th century Grade II listed pub that Polly recommended to me. From the carpark, I can see that it's as pretty as she described it, with a large glass extension and outdoor terrace overlooking extensive gardens. I'm sure that it looks wonderful in spring and summer but even now, in the late autumn, it's lovely. The leaves left on the trees and those that have fallen to the ground are red, orange, yellow and brown and a brisk wind whips the puffs of cloud across the bright blue sky.

Wrapping my thick cardigan tightly around my chest, I grab my bag then cross the car park and enter the pub. Aromas of garlic and tomato greet me and my mouth waters. Polly said the food here is delicious and I'm glad I skipped breakfast now to leave room lunch.

Nala waves at me from the bar and I hurry over to her. We've spoken on the phone but I haven't seen her in person since the day when she told me about the nannying contract and I've missed her. We hug then she stands back and appraises me.

'You look good, Ava. Country life is clearly agreeing with you.'

'Do you think so?'

She nods. 'You have colour in your cheeks and you look... rested. Happy.'

'It's a good job.'

She tilts her head to one side. 'It's more than that, though. I've known you a while now and I've never seen your eyes shine so brightly.'

Laughing, I lean my arm on the bar and look at the bottles attached to the optics. The memory of being at The Shard flashes before my eyes and then, of Edward on his knees in front of me, removing my shoes, moving his hand up my leg. My heart pounds and I force the image away. I've tried so hard not to think about it, but it's been a long time since I've slept with anyone. Marriage to him would offer financial stability but could it possibly offer a physical connection as well? But not love. Could I have sex without love?

*It wouldn't be the first time...*But that was different. I was younger and had no idea what I wanted or needed; it was done for the wrong reasons entirely.

Nala places a hand on my arm. 'I think you have things to share with me, Ava. I can tell that there's something on your mind. You know you can trust me, right?'

'I know that.' I meet her eyes and smile. 'It's just... quite a lot to get my head around.'

'Well let's get some drinks and go and find a table then you can tell me all about it.'

When we're sitting at a table near the window in the

extension that overlooks the rear garden. I take a deep breath. 'To be honest, Nala, I feel like I'm stuck inside a movie or something.'

'Ooh, is it like *Pretty Woman,* but without the prostitution obviously, or *Fifty Shades of Grey,* but without the BDSM. Unless that's your thing, obviously. BDSM not prostitution! Sorry, I'm babbling in my excitement. So go on, tell me! I'll be quiet now, I promise.'

She feigns zipping her lips, leans her elbows on the table and rests her chin on her hands. I tell her about the grand house with its numerous rooms. About Joe and how much I adore him. I tell her about Polly and Jeff and how kind they've been to me. I describe what life is like there with vast lawns just outside the house and an orchard where I can while away the hours walking, sitting and reading, even on colder days. When it's cooler, I can wrap myself in a coat and blankets and go and sit there with a flask of tea or hot chocolate. I have never been able to take time to just exist in the moment and it is wonderful, heavenly in fact. Nala was right; I do feel better than I ever have done. Healthier. Fitter. More relaxed. The Buckinghamshire air is fresh and clean and I'm in better health than I've ever been. And I know that I could give all this to Mum and Daniel if I just accept Edward's proposal.

'It sounds amazing.' Nala nods. 'I'm so glad you're enjoying it.'

'The time is flying past though.' My tone is tainted with regret. It's almost November and then I'll have just two months left until the end of the contract. I'll have to go back to our small flat and to the life I had before. And yes, I miss Mum and Daniel so much but what I don't miss was the drudgery of life there, the lack of open space that I have freely at my disposal now. The thought of leaving is dreadful because I'll have to leave Polly and Jeff, Joe and... Edward. And while he might never be mine in the traditional sense of a husband, he could be my husband and I'd get to stay in his home and to bring my family there. Our life could be incredible in so many ways if I'm prepared to take a chance.

'There's more,' I say, then I sigh. 'What would you do if you were offered an opportunity to change your life?'

'Would it be for the better?' Nala asks.

'On the whole, yes.'

'Can you be more specific?'

'In strictest confidence?'

'Always. You know I'm not a blabber mouth.' She waggles her eyebrows at me.

I tug my cardigan sleeves down over my hands because my fingers are cold even though the pub is warm and I drag air deep into my lungs before replying.

'Edward has asked me to marry him.'

Her mouth falls open and the shock on her face makes me laugh out loud. A few people at other tables glance over and I lower my head, stare at the sleeves covering my hands to avoid meeting anyone's eyes.

'Say what?'

'Edward has asked me to be his wife.'

'But... I thought... you guys... I'm don't understand.' Her knitted brows are proof of her confusion, so I fill her in on the details of the proposal and what it would involve, at least what I know so far as we haven't discussed the finer details of what the marriage of convenience would be like, and she nods, not interrupting once until I'm done.

I sip my drink while I wait for her to respond. She's picked up a beer mat and is tearing it into tiny pieces that she drops onto the table, and it makes me think of confetti.

If I play this right, I could have a wedding but if I play it wrong and fall for Edward, my heart could be broken into as many pieces as that beer mat.

'OK, Ava. I have one question and I think it's the most important one.'

'Ask away.'

'How do you feel about the proposal?'

I sigh then sit back in my seat letting my hands emerged from my sleeves.

'Confused?' It comes out as a question.

'You're not sure if you're confused or you are confused?'

'Both.'

'Edward Cavendish is a good-looking man. That's undeniable. But you've only known him for what... ten weeks or so?'

'Some people have whirlwind romances.' I shrug.

'That's true but is this in any way a romance? Are you two... making the beast with two backs?'

'The what beast?'

Nala rubs her cheeks. 'Are you sleeping together?'

'Oh! No, no. Not at all.'

'Well then... are you in love?'

'Nope.'

'But he wants to marry you?'

'He does. As I told you, it'll be a business deal.'

'So only as a deal?' Her frown deepens. 'A marriage of convenience,' she tests the words out.

'I guess so.'

She purses her lips. 'Look... Ava, I care about you and I want to see you happy. I know how you've struggled over the years and this would ease your financial worries. There would be no more fretting about money if you marry a billionaire, that's for sure.'

'Exactly.'

'But I'm guessing that there would be a prenup? You know, so that you couldn't take him for every penny a few years down the line.'

'I would think so and hopefully that also protects me.'

'Right. So if you do separate, you'll have a guaranteed lump sum?'

'If we do or don't separate. I think I get something either way.'

She gazes out of the window and I look at her profile, wondering what she would do in my shoes.

'So,' she says, turning back to me, 'You'd be looked after.'

'For the first time ever.'

'Oh Ava.' She reaches across the table and squeezes my hand. 'It's a difficult one because I know how hard you work and I know that you can do so much with your intelligence and abilities. From a feminist perspective I want to shout that you don't need a man to do all that. But... this isn't about needing a man, it's about opportunity and Edward is offering you a business opportunity. If it was me... and a gorgeous billionaire asked me to marry him, I'd give it some serious thought.' She smiles at me. 'But... is it going to be strictly business for you both?'

I lick my lips and take my time before I reply. 'I think so.'

'There's more?' she asks. 'If you search your soul, can you tell if there are feelings involved too?'

'I'm not sure. We had a... a moment on my birthday and there were definitely sparks on my part. But I don't know if he's like that with all women and if it was just because we'd had a few drinks and... I honestly don't know for sure. I haven't been with a man in years and, as you said, Edward is gorgeous. I'm only human, after all.'

'If you two find that there's more between you than strictly business then that would be perfect. Kind of like a fairy tale.' She raises her glass. 'Look... don't rush. See how things go over the next few weeks and then make your decision. I think that as long as everything's signed and sealed, and you're protected financially then it could be a good thing for you. And, of course, for your mum and Daniel.'

'Exactly. Just think how their lives could be improved.'

'They could. But your mum and Daniel will want you to be happy. That matters more to them than where they live and how much they have to spend on things.'

'I know. There's also Joe to think about. I'm growing very fond of him. If I marry Edward, I could be there to help raise him.'

She sits back and folds her arms. 'What about... other aspects of a marriage though? Like... I know you said you're not sleeping with Edward right now but would you share a room after the wedding? Would you...' She waggles her eyebrows and heat crawls up my throat and into my cheeks.

'I'm not sure.' Somehow, I doubt that a business arrangement of this kind would involve sex and I'm kind of disappointed by that thought. And then I'm kind of embarrassed that I'm feeling that way. Who even am I now?

'Do you like him enough to go there though?'

Edward's eyes pinning me to the chair. His hand sliding up my leg. My whole body responding and wanting him to touch me... That deep thrumming at my core than made me clench inside and year to feel him possessing my body.

'I think I could.'

'As long as he's kind to you, go for it. But please take care of yourself because no one wants to see you hurt.'

No one wants to see me hurt. That's one thing I am worried about. What if I develop deep feelings for him and he just sees this as business. He could be one of those men who can have sex without emotion involved. I could do that too, I suppose, but I'm already more involved in all of this than I'd have liked. The idea of being his wife is growing on me and I need to be careful not to become too fond of him. He's lost one wife and has told me that he doesn't want a proper marriage, so this really is a case of putting on my business head and not allowing my emotions to get tangled.

'You're a good friend, Nala. Thanks for listening.'

'Anytime, honey. And if you accept his proposal and need help with any of the wedding planning let me know, although I'm sure Edward has plenty of contacts he can call on for that. Shall we have another drink?'

I nod and Nala heads to the bar. Nothing about my situation or Edward's proposal is simple and things have the potential to get messy, but as long as I protect my heart, it will all work out fine.

Won't it?

Chapter 29

Ava

When I got home yesterday, I went for a walk around the grounds. Mum Facetimed me so I showed her where I was, and she got emotional. She said it was because she was glad that I'm staying in such a beautiful location, but I suspect part of it was also her worrying about me having to leave here after the nannying contract ends. It added to my thoughts that marrying Edward could be a good thing for us all. The damp in the flat doesn't help with her health struggles and I'm sure it's affecting Daniel. I know that I'll have enough money from this job to buy a new place, but I also know that money doesn't go far these days. Without doing more qualifications, I'll never be able to get a better paid job and to be honest, I'll never get one that will make the kind of difference that marrying Edward could make. Also, if I marry Edward I could afford to do more qualifications, perhaps start a business of my own. There will, for the first time in my life, be options open for me.

Being on the land here, breathing the fresh air and being close to Edward and Joe, it's starting to feel normal, like this is my life. Would being his wife really be that different to how things are now? Yes, I know, there would be some differences, but I'd be able to stay here, close to them both. The thought of leaving them is starting to make me anxious and I know I'd miss them, as well as Polly and Jeff.

After my walk, I went inside, and Edward and Joe were there. Joe hugged me and asked me to go and play with his Lego. I was about to follow him when Edward asked me for a quick chat. He said that he'd agreed to go to a pumpkin carving competition at the village hall this evening and asked if I'd go too. He's sponsoring the event and the money will go to a local charity that helps out elderly people in need, the ones who don't have family around. It organises meals at the village hall for them as well as social gatherings. It made me think about how many people ask him for his time and money and about how I've never heard him complain about it. He was born into money but he also works hard for it and yet I've never seen him begrudge anyone a penny or some of his time and that endears him to me even more. He has a good heart, and it makes me want to spend more time with him.

And so I agreed to go this evening but I warned him that I am pretty ace at carving pumpkins. He laughed but he's got no idea what's coming...

Chapter 30

Edward

I end the business call then go to the kitchen to grab a coffee. Just outside the door, I hear giggling, so I pause and listen. It's Ava and Joe.

'Let me try, Ava!' Joe says.

'OK but be caref— Ah! Joe! Look what you've done!'

More giggling. What on earth are they doing in there?

I walk into the kitchen and the sight that greet me stops me in my tracks. They are at the kitchen table, Joe standing on a chair, Ava next to him and they're both covered in flour. They're wearing aprons but even so, Joe has flour in his hair, on his face and up his arms. Ava has flour in her hair and on her face too. They look up and grin at me.

'What's going on in here?' I ask. 'You look like ghosts.'

'Ha ha! Daddy said we're ghosts, Ava.' Joe grins at her. 'Daddy, Ava said we could do baking to take to the party,' Joe says, rubbing a hand over his forehead and leaving a smear of what looks like orange icing there.

'We're making some Halloween muffins to take, with us,' Ava explains. 'And we're *trying* to decorate them.' She nods at Joe and smiles.

'We used punkin puree, Daddy.' Joe blinks at me.

'Punkin eh?' I nod and go to have a closer look. 'They smell great.'

Peering at them, I have to admit that they look pretty good too. They've decorated the muffins with different coloured icing and added what look like pumpkin faces to some, spider legs to others and the rest have white ghost shapes on them with hollow black eyes.

'Wow! You have been busy.' I smile at Ava and she blushes through the flour. Whenever she does that, I find it so cute. It makes me want to grab hold of her and hug her. Especially now that she's all covered in flour and looking more adorable than ever.

'Would you like one?' Ava asks.

'Yes please. Which one can I have?'

Joe peruses the muffins then selects one and holds it out. 'Have this one, Daddy.'

It's a ghost muffin. I peel back the orange paper case and take a bite. 'Mmmm.' I'm not exaggerating; it's good. Really good. 'Delicious!'

'Daddy likes them!' Joe's smile makes my heart leap. I try not to dwell on it but I do worry about him since we lost Lucille. He's so young to be without his mum and although he's had Cynthia around, and she's amazing, she's more like a grandmother than a mother figure. But Ava, well, she's young and energetic and she's a natural with Joe. The thought of losing her from our lives now is getting tough to deal with and I hope she's going to accept my proposal and stay.

'I'm glad Daddy likes them.' Ava is smiling at Joe, but as she finishes speaking, she looks at me and something in her eyes makes my heart hammer.

Once I've finished the muffin, I wash my hands, dry

them then return to the table. 'Right you two, I don't want to spoil the fun but we've got to go in a hour and you need to... uh... get cleaned up.'

Ava looks down at herself and seems surprised at the state of her apron then she raises a hand to her face and looks at her palm. 'Oh dear!'

'Yeah... you've got some flour there.' I point at her hair and she raises her hand covering it with even more flour and grimaces. 'Oops! Your Daddy is right, Joe, we should go and get showered.'

'I'll sort Joe out while you sort yourself.'

'Are you sure?'

'Absolutely.' I nod. We do need to get going soon and I don't want her to have to rush.

'Thanks, Edward.'

I give them a hand to tidy up the kitchen then take Joe up to shower. While I help him to shampoo his hair then rinse it clean, he chats about how much he loves being with Ava and I can't help thinking that I do too.

Chapter 31

Ava

When we get to the village hall, driven there by Jeff because it's a bit of a trek across fields to walk there from the house, it looks amazing. The large garden out front is decorated with all sorts of Halloween paraphernalia like fake spider webs, pumpkin bunting, carved pumpkins, white satin ghosts that have been hung from the trees and some of those animated talking figures that react whenever someone walks past them. Joe squeals as a creepy-looking witch gives an ominous cackle as he passes it and he grabs my hand. I can only hope it doesn't give him nightmares.

Inside the hall, the main room has stalls set up around the periphery then at the centre of the wooden floor is a large trestle table with some — as yet — untouched pumpkins and carving tools. My stomach gives a flip of anticipation because this is where the carving will take place and I'm going to be a part of it.

'What do you want to do first?' Edward asks.

'We should take those to the cake stall,' I say, nodding at the tray in his arms.

'Of course.' He smiles. 'Then what?'

'Can we go and look at the books, Daddy?' Joe asks, pointing at a stall.

'Books?' Edward laughs. 'Of course we can.'

Once we've dropped the cakes off, we go to the second-hand books stall and Edward lifts Joe up so he can see properly. I browse some of the romance titles available, glancing at Edward and Joe from time to time because I love seeing their bond. Edward is such a good dad and Joe loves him deeply. I don't recall my own father ever spending time with me like that and he was barely around for Daniel. Some people shouldn't have children. It's one of the reasons why I never thought to have children myself. I've always been afraid of what type of parent I'd be. My mum is wonderful but my father, well, he absented himself mentally and emotionally from our lives even before he walked out the door that final time and never came back. I can't imagine Edward ever doing that to Joe but I've always held a fear that one day, if I had children, I might let them down the way my father let me and Daniel down. After all, how far does the apple fall from the tree?

'A lot of these books are actually brand new,' the woman standing behind the stall says to me. 'They've been donated by local authors.'

It occurs to me that Edward might have had something to do with that. He probably knows lots of famous people.

'Are they signed too?' I ask.

'They are.' She picks up a novel from an author I know well, and I take a look.

'Well then, I can't resist.'

'What can't you resist?' Edward asks.

'Signed books.' I show him the novel.

Meeting the Billionaire Boss

'Let me get that for you.' He takes it and hands it to the stallholder. 'And whatever else she wants.'

It's strange for me when he takes control like this. Part of me, that I suspect is a primitive part, enjoys it but the more modern part of me, the part that was hurt by my dad leaving, screams at me to run for the hills. I try to relax into the experience and to give it time because I'm sure it's just who Edward is, and I'd like to see where it leads. Plus I'm inclined to think that Edward does this instinctively; it's in his nature to take care of others. If two people are in a relationship, surely they do take care of each other and take the lead in different situations, so perhaps it's natural for me to enjoy Edward's behaviour. I'm so inexperienced with men that I just don't know.

The woman nods and puts the book in a bag along with the ones that Joe has chosen.

'You're a lucky woman,' she says quietly to me and I'm about to tell her that Edward isn't my man, is in fact my boss, but something stops me. Instead, I go to Edward and Joe, and Joe slides his small arm around my neck. Edward is still holding him, so it means that the three of us are brought close together. It feels good.

'I love you, Daddy and Ava,' Joe says suddenly. He pulls me closer, and I end up putting out a hand to steady myself. It lands on Edward's hard chest and I can feel his steady heartbeat beneath the material of his shirt.

Edward replies, 'We love you too, Joe.'

'Hug Ava, Daddy,' Joe says with the innocence of a child wanting the people he cares about to be close.

Edward shrugs apologetically at me then slides his arm around my back and the three of us stand in a mini group hug. I'm conscious of Joe's hand in my hair. Of Edward's body warm and close to me. Of everywhere we are connected. Of how much I care about these two and how much I wish this was real, that we were actually a little family.

'Hello! Hello! What's going on here then?'

At the question, Edward releases me and I step back.

'Hey guys, what's happening?' It's Edward's friend and business partner, Lucas, and he's grinning like the cat that got the cream.

'Daddy got us books,' Joe says.

'Hey champ.' Lucas holds out his arms and Joe goes to him, wrapping his arms around Lucas's neck.

'Hi, Uncle Lucas.'

While the men talk, I wander off and browse the stalls, buying myself a moment to breathe and think as much as because I want to see what's on offer. As well as the book stall, there's a stall selling cakes, one selling jams, honey and pickles and another selling local craft gin and fruit wine. Some of it sounds delicious and what's even more impressive is that it's all organic. I buy a few things and put them into the tote bag I brought. I'm looking at some olive oil containing herbs when something catches my eye across the hall.

A woman has arrived and she's attracting quite a bit of attention. I have no idea who she is but suspect she could be a local celebrity or even a national one. The thing with ignoring social media is that I'm often oblivious to who's *up and coming* these days. As she sashays across the hall like she owns it then stands next to Edward and Lucas., I can't take my eyes off her. She's like an exotic bird or perhaps more like a predatory big cat as she lays a proprietorial hand on Edward's arm. It suggests familiarity, ownership, confidence. My stomach lurches and I turn away, reprimanding myself for not being prepared for something like this.

Edward is bound to have a plethora of female admirers and plenty of interest from them too. After all, he's one of the country's most eligible bachelors.

'Ava!' Joe runs to me, and I scoop him up and hold him close. 'Don't like that lady,' he says into my neck.

I swallow down my reply that I don't like her either, trying not to stare at how territorial she is as she slides an arm around Edward's back, her long, red nails like talons, then laughs loudly. If I had any doubts about my place in Edward's life, I'm being reminded of it now.

Chapter 32

Edward

Being polite is in my DNA. It's how I was raised and a rule of business, but it's still hard not to pull away when I feel Flo Montague's arm snake its way around my back. Joe has run over to Ava, his juvenile intuition telling him that Flo isn't genuine. I wish I could follow my son and be with Ava too, but this is a village event and social manners dictate that I have to be *sociable*.

Florence - or Flo as she calls herself now – is a social media influencer. Born to one of England's wealthy families, she sailed through school without needing to obtain excellent qualifications and set herself up as an Instagram star. All sorts of companies send her things so she'll post about them on her grid and she does so with aplomb. I've nothing against Flo or what she does but she made it clear some time ago that she'd set her sights on me and has done her best over the years to seduce me. Unfortunately for her, I have zero romantic interest in her and wish she wouldn't be so tactile. But I also know there are cameras following her every move and so I don't spurn her publicly or show my distaste for her attention. The main reason I grit my teeth though is because her father and grandfather are on the Board of Directors at Cavendish Construction and being rude to her would not endear me to them. It does occur to me now though that a bride would also come in useful as a way to keep Flo away. A cunning move to get the message across that I'm not interested in her while not disturbing the status quo with her family.

'So, darling, what are the plans for this evening?' she asks.

'There's plenty arranged,' I reply, slipping a finger beneath my collar to ease the building pressure there.

'And I'm happy to entertain you,' Lucas grins at Flo but she stares at him as if he has two heads.

'I want Edward to entertain me.' She presses herself against my side and I try not to squirm. The problem with Flo is that she only wants me because she can't have me. Lucas would shag her up against the wall outside right now if she was up for it but she's not interested. That would be too easy. She wants me because I'm a challenge. I have no doubt that if she got me, she'd soon lose interest.

'I uhhh... need to go and see to Joe,' I say, glancing over at Ava who's cuddling my son as she talks calmly to him. I wonder what she's saying and if he needed reassurance. Something inside me cries out that I want her reassurance too.

'Let's get some photos done first then you can go to him.' Flo removes her arm from my back and takes my hand then leads me outside. I glance back one more time to check on Joe and I catch Ava watching me, something in her eyes that looks like hurt.

Outside, very reluctantly, I pose for the minimum amount of photos and selfies that I can stand, then Flo has some photos done with locals who clearly know her from social media. She's gracious enough with them but I can tell that her smile isn't genuine. The way her eyes flit over them as if they're beneath her makes something rise inside me and a bitter taste fills my mouth. Flo is a product of society and culture and so it's not entirely her fault that she's the way she is but she does have to take some of the blame. She sails around, vacantly creating this façade of a perfect life and a perfect world, but the reality is that she's fake from her frozen forehead to her lips and her teeth, as well as to other body parts I'd prefer not to think about. I knew her before she got all the cosmetic work done and she was a pretty young woman back then. Now, she looks like a doll, and while some men like that, it's not my thing at all. My fear for Flo is that she'll keep having work done to appear young, not realising that overdoing it with cosmetic surgery merely leads to people looking strange instead of ageing normally.

While Flo is distracted by a teenaged girl asking for career advice, I seize my chance and slip back inside the hall to seek out Ava and Joe. I find them sitting in a quiet corner, one of the books Joe wanted open on his lap as Ava reads to him. For a long time, I've felt stiff and brittle, as if I'll crack if I don't keep myself rigid inside. But seeing them like this, something inside me gives a little, kind of like a coil loosening. Ava takes such good care of Joe and again, it occurs to me that if anything ever happened to me, I'd want someone there to care for him. To love him like I do.

Could that person be right in front of me now?

Chapter 33

Ava

Edward is back and relief rushes through me like warm spiced wine as I meet his gaze. Joe didn't like that woman at all and I needed to distract him so we found a quiet spot to read one of his new books. When Edward went outside with her, I felt queasy and I had to force myself to shake it off. I have no right to want Edward to avoid women like that, women who make me feel like there's something wrong with me. Like I'm inadequate in some way. It was like the popular girls at school who looked down their noses at me and made me feel like I wasn't worthy of their friendship. With my second-hand uniform and cheap shoes, my old bag and lack of makeup, I was anathema to them. Instead of taking pity on me, they bullied me and their mocking still rings in my ears some days. It's hard to put that type of hurt behind you but I've done my best to move on because I know that living in the past is a waste of today. The thing I have struggled most to deal with is the hurt and betrayal of my father leaving, but even that is something I strive to push aside. I refuse to let it affect the woman I am now and the woman I want to be.

Edward crouches down in front of us and says, 'You both OK?'

I nod but Joe replies, 'Don't like that lady, Daddy.'

Edward crinkles his nose. 'I know, Joe, but she's helping with the event. She brings a lot of publicity to things, which is obviously important in today's culture,' he says to me. 'She's an influencer.'

'Oh.' No wonder I don't know her.

'She's like an 18th cousin of the King once removed or something like that. Apparently has a link to Edward III via his son, John of Gaunt. Although it was the reality TV dating show that catapulted her to stardom and since then she's done several more similar shows. To be honest, the royal connections are so distant that it's the reality TV show that's given her celebrity status.'

I have no idea who he's talking about, but I incline my head as if I do. What I do understand though is that this woman has a sense of entitlement. Hence the confidence that I could never emulate.

'Is the book good?' Edward asks.

'I think so,' I say, leaning forwards and peering over Joe's shoulder. 'Joe seemed to enjoy the story.'

'Daddy, can I have a dog?' Joe asks.

'A dog?' Edward frowns.

'In the story the boy gets a dog and they become best friends.'

'It's true,' I say.

'Let me have a think about it.' Edward stands up. 'It's almost time for the pumpkin carving competition.'

'Excellent.' I slide Joe off my lap and stand up then put Joe's book back in the bag.

'Lucas will watch Joe while we compete.' Edward looks

around the hall. 'There he is. Come on, Joe, let's get you settled so you can enjoy the show.'

As they walk away, I take a deep breath and prepare to show off my skills. My thoughts stray to my brother. Will he be trying to carve his own pumpkin this evening or will Mum try to do it for him? I miss them both so much but I also feel like my world is changing. I haven't let anyone else in for years and but now, the Cavendish men are gaining space in my heart.

And you know what? It absolutely terrifies me.

As I work on the pumpkin, I'm conscious of Edward nearby. He's rolled up his shirt sleeves and it's hard to ignore his buff forearms, the ripple of the muscles of his back as he works because his shirt has been stretched over his broad shoulders. I'm impressed by how seriously he's taking this and by the fact that despite his wealth and how busy he is, he's prepared to give his time to a local event like this. It shows that he's so much more than a driven businessman. I remind myself that I need to focus because there's a time limit and we don't have long left.

When the whistle sounds to end the competition, I push the back of my hand across my forehead. I'm warm and my cheeks feel flushed, but I think I've done a good job.

Edward looks across at me and his eyes widen. 'Wow! You really are talented.'

'Didn't I warn you?' I wiggle my eyebrows. This is fun.

'Now it's time for the judges to score the pumpkins.' The man, who is apparently a local councillor, waves an arm and the group of judges approach the table. With dismay, I see that the woman who was pawing Edward is among them, and she has eyes only for him. I don't think I'm going to stand a chance.

There are eight pumpkins to judge and I'm last but one. The judges get to Edward and assess his efforts and then it's my turn. The woman, I think Edward called her Flo, stares at me, then at my pumpkin and her upper lip wrinkles slightly. She's clearly not impressed.

'What's that meant to be?' she asks.

'Isn't it obvious?' Edward cuts across her. 'It's a dog's face.'

'A dog?' Flo tilts her head then shakes it vigorously. 'Can't see it.'

'Perhaps you need glasses.' Edward rolls his eyes at me.

I look at his pumpkin and have to admit that it's a good effort. He's carved an owl on the pumpkin and it's perched on the branch of a tree.

As the judges go to the next contestant, I pick up a paper towel and clean off my hands.

'Yours is brilliant,' Edward says. 'Did you do that specially for Joe?'

'I did. I was going to carve something different but when he asked for a dog, I thought he'd like this more.'

'He will.' The look Edward gives me makes my knees weak and I break eye contact. How can he give me all the feels with just his eyes?

When the judges walk away to confer, Joe and Lucas come over to us.

'Great effort, you two,' Lucas says. 'You clearly have some skills in common.' There's something in his crooked grin and the sparkle in his piercing blue gaze that oozes mischief. What exactly is he implying here?

'I think so.' Edward pats his trouser pocket as if he's

checking something's there then he narrows his eyes at Lucas and Lucas gives a brief nod.

What's going on?

Flo's voice cuts through my thoughts as the results of the carving are announced.

Chapter 34

Edward

I didn't want to win and I'm pretty sure that my victory is down to Flo *influencing* the other judges, but it doesn't really matter because it's just a village competition. I wanted Ava to win because she deserves to and because it would be good for her. She doesn't seem to have a lot of confidence and I find that I want to build her up and help her to see what an incredible person she is. But before I can speak to her, Flo has my arm and we're in front of the cameras again. This type of PR is exhausting and even though I know it's necessary to keep her on side because of her relatives, I hate it. Across the hall, I see Ava go to Joe and Lucas and then they wait until the publicity is done. I'm glad Flo knows that she needs to keep the cameras away from my son.

Flo keeps hold of me like she's afraid to let go again in case I slink off and I'm parched by the time she's finished being interviewed. Ironic really seeing as how she didn't carve anything, but she has that ability to turn any situation into her own. As a businessman, I can't help but admire that, but as a human being, she irks me. She's so self-obsessed and it can't be a healthy way to live. Then again though, I wasn't exactly living a very healthy existence before Ava entered our lives like a breath of fresh spring air that cleaned out the house and cast everything in a vibrant, golden light.

'I'm going to grab a drink outside,' I say to Flo and she pouts up at me.

'Edward, when are we going to do this?' Her blue eyes peer out from behind impossibly long and thick black lashes. They make me think of hairy spider legs and I shudder, which she notices. 'Am I that repugnant to you?'

'It's not that.' I don't want to fuck her, but I also don't want to hurt her or have her turn her family against me. I need every positive vote I can get on the board. Even if I get married, I still need to have people on side going forwards or managing the business could become a lot more challenging.

'Then what?' She looks over at Ava and a small gasp escapes from between her glossy lips. 'You're not into *her*, are you? Isn't she your nanny?'

It's like Hattie all over again and makes me ashamed to be connected to people like this.

'She's Joe's nanny,' I say, firmly removing my arm from her talons now. 'And yes, I am *very much* into her.'

'But... but... she's so plain and... *dowdy*.'

I laugh and shake my head. 'Ava is beautiful and natural, funny, warm and kind. I also happen to find her hot as hell! She's the only woman for me now,' I say, then I march over to Ava, determined to follow my plan through.

I can only hope that Ava's happy to go along with it otherwise I'm going to look like a total fool.

Chapter 35

Ava

Edward storms over to us then grabs my hand. 'Shall we go and get a drink outside?'

'Oh, OK.'

'Come on, Joe.' Edward picks his son up and we leave the hall.

Outside, the air is chilly but there are heaters around the grass and the fairy lights that have been strung around the trees twinkle like stars in the darkness. I jump as one of the talking ghosts reacts to me passing and Edward and Joe laugh at me, which makes me laugh too.

There is a van parked at the kerb selling hot beverages. We go to the hatch and Edward orders a hot chocolate for Joe then asks what I want.

'I'll take a mulled cider, please.'

He orders two then pays for them.

When we have our drinks, we walk over to where hay bales have been set up on the grass in a wide circle. Edward sets Joe down on one and I sit next to him while Edward sits on the other side of him. It's chilly out here now so I wrap my hands around my cardboard cup and move closer to Joe to keep him warm.

'It's a beautiful evening.' Edward looks up and I do too.

The black canvas of the sky stretches out above us like satin pricked with silver. The moon is a pale crescent, ethereal, unfinished, a bit like I feel.

'I'm tired, Daddy.' Joe leans against Edward and yawns.

I reach into the tote bag and pull out a fleecy blanket then tuck it around Joe.

'You'll be an amazing mother one day,' Edward says.

'Perhaps.' I don't want to say that I don't want children here in front of Joe, yet it was what I always believed. But with every day that passes, I doubt my former belief a little bit more. How could I not want children when they can be as amazing as Joe?

I sip my cider and it's good, tart yet sweet, laced with cinnamon and cloves. It warms me right through and I drink it hungrily.

Joe finishes his drink, so I take his cup and set it on the ground then Edward moves him onto his lap and cradles him with one strong arm while he drinks his cider. Soon, Joe's eyelids close and he snores softly, safe in his dad's arms. It's a sight that would make even the hardest of hearts soften, and for me, it's further confirmation of my feelings for them both.

'Have you had any more thoughts about my offer?' Edward asks without looking at me. This must be difficult for him. It's important because of what it means for Joe and a part of me wants to make it all right for them. I saw how Flo behaved around Edward this evening and so I know that there are other women who'd snap him up, but are there other women who would care about Joe in the way I do? This is getting more complicated by the day because I care for them and want the best for them. In fact, I believe I could be that for them. I could secure their futures and prevent Edward having to marry someone else who might not even want Joe around. Polly mentioned this recently when we were chopping vegetables for dinner, about how someone she knows married for a second time and the new wife sent the children from the first marriage off to boarding school. The idea of little Joe being packed off alone breaks my heart and I know I can't risk that happening to him. The poor little boy has been through enough already.

'I have.'

Now Edward meets my gaze and I see his internal struggle written all over his face. This isn't easy for him and if it wasn't for the inheritance clause he probably wouldn't even consider marrying again. At least not for a while anyway.

'And?' he asks, a tiny muscle in his jaw twitching.

'I'll do it.'

'You will?'

'Yes. For you and for Joe and for my family.'

Edward looks so relieved that my eyes sting with hot tears. I'm getting too attached, but I can't seem to help myself. This man could well be my undoing.

'Thank you.' He puts his cup down and takes my hand in his. It's warm and strong and I squeeze it, trying to say a million things through my touch while not being certain about what it is I'm trying to convey. Why is it so hard to know what I want, to know what I'm feeling? I should know now, surely? And yet, this situation isn't straightforward at all. It's the most complicated situation I think a person could end up in. This man wants to marry me, but he doesn't love me. He wants to secure his son's inheritance and by marrying him I'll secure my brother's future and my mother's care going forwards should her conditions worsen. Edward is kind and caring and he makes me feel good and yet, he sees me as an employee. If only this was real, and he loved me. If only we were going into this for love and nothing else, how happy I would be. But that would be some kind of fairy tale and life isn't like that. Life is about being pragmatic and making decisions to benefit the people you love.

Edward lets go of my hand, stands up still holding Joe then pulls his phone from his pocket. He holds it up as he types with one hand and next thing I know; Jeff pulls up at the side of the village hall. Edward settles Joe in the back of the car then turns to me.

'Jeff will take him home and Polly will put him to bed. I doubt he'll even wake up.'

'It's not a problem, I can go with him.'

'Please stay,' he says. 'It's important to me that you do.'

I nod and he gently closes the door of the car and Jeff waves then gets in and drives away. It's like having paid grandparents on call because I know that Jeff and Polly adore Joe and treat him like he's family.

'Come with me?' Edward holds out his hand.

I take it, aware that I am accepting what he has to offer me, even if it's not everything I wish it could be.

Chapter 36

Edward

Inside the hall, the warmth hits me, so I remove my coat immediately then help Ava out of hers. When we walk into the main room, she gasps, and it makes me smile.

'You knew there would be a dance, didn't you?'

'I didn't realise it would be like this,' she says, looking around.

The tables have been put away and some of the hay bales brought in and set up as seating around the edges of the room. On the stage at the far end, a local band has set up and they're tuning their instruments.

'Ever do line dancing?' I ask and she shakes her head.

'Well, get ready because you're about to.'

'What?'

'Come on, let's put our things down then we can dance.'

'Edward! I don't know how.' The panic on her face makes my protective instincts stand to attention.

'I'll show you how. I'm a good teacher.' As I say the words I think about how innocent she seems at times and wonder what else I could teach her if I get the opportunity.

It's not just her age but the sheltered life she's led. I know she's worked hard and had challenging domestic circumstances, but she still has an air of naivety about her and it's adorable. It also turns me on.

We leave our coats and bags on a bale then I lead her to the centre of the hall and show her how to stand. When the music starts, she looks at me uncertainly, so I show her what to do. She soon gets the hang of it, and I find it hard to keep my eyes off her as she swings her hips and gets into the flow of the music. The smile on her face and the flush in her cheeks are enough to drive me crazy and I actually stumble over my steps a few times because I can't focus properly.

When the song ends, I pull her to me and whisper into her ear, 'Where have you been all my life?'

I must confess that I'm struggling not to develop feelings for her. In fact, despite my intention to keep this strictly business, I want to make her mine.

'What?' She blinks at me.

'You're amazing. I've never met anyone like you.'

Before I can say more, the next song starts and I pull her in front of me and place my hands on her waist, feeling the swell of her hips lower down, aware that if I were to slide my hands upwards they could cup her full breasts. It makes me breathless with desire and I glance around us to distract myself. Other people are lost in the dancing, laughing and singing along as they count their steps, and I push my thoughts about touching Ava inappropriately away.

After a few upbeat dances, the music changes and the band plays a version of Chris Isaak's *'Two Hearts'*. I hold out my hands and Ava takes them then we dance, my one hand on her waist, the other holding her hand tightly. When the song changes to Kenny Rogers' *'We've Got Tonight'*, I pull Ava closer then sing softly to her, meaning every word. There are no guarantees in any relationship but right now, I want this woman.

When the song finishes, I look up and spot Lucas watching us from across the room. He gives me a thumbs up and I nod.

It's time.

I take a step back and gaze at Ava, trying to capture this moment in my memory while I know that Lucas is capturing it on camera for the board. If they have any doubts about my engagement then they can see the video evidence of what I hope will be a romantic and genuine looking proposal. A sudden wedding in May would spark questions but an engagement now in October then a spring wedding should be enough to convince them. To keep my business and secure my future and that of Joe, I'll do anything.

Slowly, I drop to one knee. All around us, the hall falls silent. Ava's eyes widen and her jaw drops as I take her hand.

'Ava Thorne...'

Chapter 37

Ava

I can't believe what's happening when Edward drops to one knee. It's like I'm dreaming and at any moment I'm going to wake up. I know people are staring at us and my introvert side wants to run and hide from all these curious eyes but it's like I'm rooted to the spot and I couldn't move even if I wanted to. But I don't really want to. I want to find out what Edward is going to say.

'Ava Thorne...'

'Yes?'

'Will you do me the great honour of becoming my wife?'

I look up and all around us people are smiling, some pressing their hands to their chests, others already getting phones out to capture the moment. I guess it's not every day the local billionaire proposes to his son's nanny at the village hall. Even so, concern fill me because I know Edward doesn't want people prying into his life. But then again, if this is to convince the board that our relationship is real then I can see how it could be an important step.

'Ava?'

I return my gaze to Edward. He looks so handsome and yet so vulnerable waiting there for my answer.

I nod then reply, 'Yes. Of course I'll marry you.'

He slides one hand into his trouser pocket and brings out a ring.

'Oh my god!' I stare at the platinum band as he slides it onto my ring finger. It's studded with diamonds and has a huge square diamond at the centre surrounded by even more diamonds. It's the most beautiful ring I've ever seen and must have cost a fortune. 'That's for me?'

'Of course it's for you.' He kisses my hand then stands up and opens his arms. I step into his embrace and he holds my gaze, gently tilts my chin then lowers his head and kisses me.

All around me, I hear claps and cheers but all I can focus on is how good his lips feel against mine. How incredible his body feels as it presses close to me and how much I want him to take me home. I slide my arms around his neck and kiss him back and he moans softly against my lips, making my entire body hum with longing.

When he finally breaks away, I could cry with disappointment but then I'm suddenly aware of our audience so I straighten my shirt and run my hands through my hair while Edward accepts the congratulations being showered upon him.

'I think it's time for champagne,' Edward says, pointing across the room. I follow his finger to see Lucas carrying a tray of glasses while three other men carry bottles of what I'm sure is a very expensive bubbly.

The rest of the evening passes in a blur as I'm congratulated by numerous people and they admire the ring then tell me how lucky I am. And yes, I am lucky, but not in the way they think because while this all seems like a fairy tale come true, I know deep down that there won't be a happy ending.

After all, in real life, when does Cinderella get to marry the handsome prince and live happily ever after?

Chapter 38

Ava

The next morning, I wake alone. I went to bed alone last night so I don't know why I thought it would be any different. We came home from the village hall exhausted after all the excitement and Edward went to his study while I went straight to bed. I think I had hoped that we might at least kiss again after that incredible kiss following the proposal, but then, it was all fake so why would we?

I stretch out in bed, appreciating the sheer comfort of this enormous bed, along with the freshly laundered Egyptian cotton sheets and I catch sight of the enormous diamond on my finger. It really is gorgeous, and I take a moment to admire it. Surely any woman would be delighted to receive an engagement ring of that size and quality? But then a woman who'd just got engaged would also probably expect to wake up next to her fiancé.

And I am here alone.

There's no point feeling sorry for myself though because that won't achieve anything, so I get up and wash, dress and head downstairs. It's still early, just after six, and I have time before Joe needs to get up, so I go to the kitchen and find Polly there.

'Good morning, lovely.' She smiles at me then her eyes go to my left hand. 'Congratulations are in order, I hear.'

I smile and hold out my hand but I feel bad. The last thing I want to do is deceive this lovely woman but what can I do? When we left the village hall last night and went outside to wait for Jeff to collect us, Edward told me that our engagement would need to seem real for everyone, staff included. I did ask about the separate beds thing but he said not to worry as he often works late and so that can be easily explained as him not wanting to disturb me. We both need to sleep and we're not married yet so he said it will be fine.

'That's a beauty.' Polly takes my hand and moves it from side to side. 'He must love you a lot to get you a ring like that.'

I meet her eyes and I think I see doubt there but I don't explain myself. Even if she knows, she's too polite to say and so it's better to maintain the façade that the engagement is real. But then Polly says, 'Ava... I know that you came here as a nanny and I know that things might not be... conventional for you and Edward, but I do think this could be a positive thing. I've seen Edward go through a very tough time, he was terribly low in fact, but since you arrived, he's been different. What you two do is your business, obviously, but I wanted you to know that I do love having you around. You fit in here and Joe clearly adores you.'

I nod, not knowing how to reply.

'What I'm trying to say... is that things have a way of working out.' She places a hand on my arm and before I know what I'm doing, I hug her.

She laughs and pats my back.

'It will all be OK, sweet girl. You'll see.'

When she releases me, I sniff then say, 'Thanks, Polly. I hope so.'

'Just give him time to realise what he's got. Sometimes it takes a while, but it will happen.'

Her words make me wonder how much she understands about what's going on but I decide not to explain anything just in case I've got the wrong end of the stick and she doesn't know that my engagement is fake.

'Have you seen Edward this morning?'

A fine line appears between her brows. 'You don't know then?'

'Know what?'

'Edward left about half an hour ago. He said he's going to London and will be gone a few days..'

He's gone away? Now? Whatever for?

'I think he's gone to see his lawyer and to get some things in order,' she adds, giving my arm a pat. 'He probably has meetings too knowing Edward. Always such a busy man. Before he lost Lucille, he was always working. Those two were like ships in the night most of the time.' Her eyes widen and she shakes her head. 'I've probably said too much there so please ignore me. Can I get you some breakfast?'

'That would be great, thanks,' I say, even though my stomach feels like it's full of lead and the last thing I want is to eat right now. I help myself to coffee then sit down at the table, suddenly exhausted. Why didn't he tell me he was going away? Will it always be like this with me left wondering if he cares at all?

If so, it's going to be tougher than I anticipated being married to Edward Cavendish.

Chapter 39

Edward

Leaving before Ava woke this morning was probably cowardly of me but I knew I couldn't trust myself to see her again so soon. When we got home last night, I wanted to take her to bed and make love to her but that would have confused things so instead I went to my study and locked the door. I turned on my computer and tried to focus but all I could think about was how it had felt to kiss Ava's soft lips, how holding her against me had stirred me and how a fake engagement was going to be more of a challenge than I'd anticipated.

The moment when I'd pulled her to me and kissed her kept playing over and over in my mind. Her lips had parted beneath mine. Her body had yielded, shaped itself to mine and damn... it was hot! Just thinking about it now is arousing me and I'm on my way to see the family lawyer so I need to calm down.

The lawyer has a marriage contract drafted because he's known since Grandpa passed away that it might be required. Now we need to firm up some things and I want to make sure that everything is as advantageous as possible for Ava. To be fair, when I first discussed the possibility of me marrying just to fulfil the inheritance clause with our lawyer, I thought I'd marry someone as a purely business transaction. I couldn't imagine ever caring for another woman like I cared for Lucille. But this is Ava, for crying out loud, and I'm already in too deep for comfort.

I'll be in the city for a few days because I have some business meetings too, and it's probably a good thing. I need some space from Ava before I do something I'll regret that will confuse the hell out of the two of us.

Never before has a business deal been so close to becoming personal. Never before have I wanted to mix business with pleasure.

What the fuck am I going to do?

Chapter 40

Ava

Edward doesn't come home for ten days.

Ten days!

If it wasn't for the engagement ring that must weigh at least a pound, I'd wonder if it had happened at all. I'm kept busy in that time by Joe, as well as by Polly and Jeff. It's like they can sense that I'm at a loss and so they encourage me to eat with them in the evenings, to bake with Joe, and Polly even takes me grocery shopping a few times to get me out of the house. They really are like adoptive parents looking out for my welfare and I'm grateful to them for their kindness. Edward does see Joe though, he takes him out for dinner several times after school then Jeff brings Joe home while Edward returns to the city. But I don't see him and it's hard.

I do get two text messages from Edward informing me that he's with the lawyer working out some aspects of the contract and to check that I'm happy with some of the things he's prepared to offer me should we, at some point in the future, decide to divorce. It's shitty to be thinking about divorce when we're not even married yet, but then I remind myself that Edward is an incredibly rich man, and he needs to protect his wealth as well as his son. Whatever happens, it sounds like I'm going to do very well out of this. At least financially and materially, that is. As for my heart, I'm not sure that it's built for this kind of transaction.

Joe is at school and I'm putting some of his toys away in his room when I hear voices. I go to the landing and peer over the banister and my heart skips a beat because there he is. Handsome as always. My fake fiancé.

As if sensing me there, he looks up and when our eyes meet, I gasp. I've missed him so much that the ache for him has been physical and it's only now that I can admit it to myself.

'See you later, Jeff.' Edward says then he turns to the stairs and climbs them two at a time.

He approaches me slowly, as if worried he'll scare me away and I gulp. There's something in his eyes and I don't know what it is, but it makes my legs shaky and my heart pound.

'Ava,' he says when he stops near me. 'Are you OK?'

'Yes. Why?'

He glances at the hallway below. 'I heard that you were... out of sorts.'

'Who—' I don't finish my question because I know it would have been Polly or Jeff who told him.

'I've got the contract with me. I want you to look over it before it's finalised and make sure that you're happy with it.'

Hunger!

That's what it is. In his eyes. He's hungry.

'OK.' I grip the banister and he glances at my hand.

'You're not OK, are you?'

I shake my head. 'I don't know. I don't understand what's happening to me.'

He closes the space between us and pulls me against his chest. He holds me so tight I can barely breathe but I hold him too. Needing him. Wanting him. Wishing things were different.

Then he lifts me in his arms and carries me to my room, pushes the door closed with his foot and lays me down on the bed. I open my mouth to speak but he shakes his head. He reaches for the button of my jeans and undoes it then the zip and next thing I know I'm naked from the waist down. I've only even been naked with one man before, a colleague I worked with at the hotel, and it didn't feel like this. It was awkward, embarrassing, forced. I did it out of curiosity and it was disappointing, nothing like the sex I'd read about. Being exposed to Edward though fills me with yearnings I can't even articulate.

'I want to taste you,' he says, holding me captive with his eyes. 'I want to make you come hard then drink you.'

Words have deserted me.

He takes my ankles and pulls me to the edge of the bed then he kneels between my legs. When he blows gently on my exposed skin, I moan. This is wrong, I know it's wrong, and yet I can't find the words to stop it.

I want it. I want him. He wants me too.

He brushes a finger over my mound then moves it in a figure of eight, each time letting the finger slide a bit lower. But he teases me, never quite touching me where I need to feel it most. My skin tingles as anticipation builds and I am so turned on I could scream.

The first brush of his tongue makes me arch my back and he takes hold of my thighs, his fingers digging into the soft flesh but this turns me on even more. He licks against me slowly, circling his tongue over my most sensitive places, a meandering caress that makes me shiver with pleasure. I slide my hands into his hair and shamelessly push him against me.

The pleasure builds and he pushes a finger inside me then another, curling them in a way that hits my G-spot and makes me breathless. His tongue speeds up and his fingers work their magic and I lose all inhibitions and move with him, moaning, begging him not to stop.

When I hurtle over the edge and come hard, I cry out his name, each ripple of ecstasy shuddering through me until I am spent.

This is what I've been missing. This is what the books and songs and poems are all about. I want to do it again and again and again.

Edward climbs up my body and lies on top of me, resting his arms either side of my head. His mouth is wet with my juices and his eyes are dark with desire.

'You are special, Ava. I don't want you to ever think otherwise.'

I can feel him hard against me, the zipper of his jeans pressing into my sensitive clit, but desire is already stirring inside me again.

'Let me make you feel good too?' My voice wavers, unsteady. I slide my hand between us and rub it over the length of him, longing to have him inside me.

He gently removes my hand and presses a kiss to my palm then he rolls off me and sits on the edge of the bed. 'I'm sorry, Ava. I can't...'

'What do you mean?'

He stands and looks down at me and I feel suddenly exposed and vulnerable, so I pull the covers over my nakedness. He rubs a hand over his face and sighs.

'I... I don't know... It's just that it's been a while and...'

Understanding washes over me then. He hasn't been with anyone since Lucille.

I shuffle towards him and take his hand in mine, pull him down to me and hold him close. He can't give that part of himself to me right now and I get that. I really do.

So we lie there together, me spooning him, stroking his head and letting him know that I'm there. I'm not going anywhere.

This man is special too.

Chapter 41

Ava

'It must be strange for you being back here after living in that lovely big house.' Mum watches me over her mug of tea.

'It is a bit but I wanted to see you both.'

Edward had asked if I wanted to go and visit Mum and Daniel before Christmas and I did, but it doesn't mean it wasn't hard to leave him and Joe. I got home late last night because I wanted to put Joe to bed before I left. When I arrived here, Mum was already sleeping on the chair so I encouraged her to go to bed then tossed and turned on the sofa all night. After having the luxury of an enormous bed all to myself, the lumpy old sofa is a shock to my system.

'Does it feel like a different world here?' Mum's switched on and she's seen the photos I've sent her since late August. There's no point in me trying to pull the wool over her eyes, although I do want to spare her feelings.

'It is different, Mum. Very different in many ways but I've missed you and Dan so much.'

'We've missed you too but you know what?' Mum nods. 'It's wonderful for me to know that you're living in that fabulous house with all that fresh air and space around you. I could never have given you all that and it makes me happy to know that you're living in a better place.'

'Mum...' I need to tell her. 'You know that the point of me taking this job in the first place was because of the brilliant salary?'

'Yes, love.'

'Well, things have changed again.'

'Oh.' I see the wariness in her eyes. She's worried that there won't be a move and a better life for Daniel. I know she doesn't care about what she goes through herself but she does care for her children and I told her I'd make life better for Dan. 'OK.'

'It's all good,' I say quickly to reassure her. 'But there's something else.'

She waits, steam rising from her milky tea. Now that I'm here, I don't know what she'll think about the idea of moving to Edward's house. She's been mistress of her own home for a long time and while I got carried away on the idea that living at Edward's would be good for her, perhaps it won't. Perhaps she won't feel like she fits in there. She's never wanted charity and only took the money I brought in because she was unable to work much herself but living in someone else's house will be completely different. Like surrendering her freedom in a way.

Is that what I'm doing?

Images of Edward flood my mind. Since that day when he came home and carried me to my room over five weeks ago, things have been different. We haven't had full sex but he has shown me physical affection in the same way many times and my desire for him has continued to grow. We've been getting on well and are almost like a little family with Joe, but I know that Edward is still holding back and it's so hard. I can't fully lower my walls unless I know he has too but sometimes I catch it in his eyes, a hesitation, the source of which he can't disclose. It saddens me to know that we might never be able to connect fully because of past hurts and fears, because we've both learnt the hard way that people can't always be trusted.

People leave. People die. Hearts can be broken. Scar tissue is tough to break down. Edward holds back physically because he's afraid to let go. Letting someone in is terrifying.

It doesn't stop me wanting him. Needing him. Craving him like he's an addiction I can't shake.

I've kept my left hand out of sight. I could have taken the ring off but I'm afraid of losing it. Now, I raise it and watch as Mum's face changes, various emotions crossing her familiar features.

'Ava... Is that what I think it is?'

I nod. I don't want to lie to Mum but I can't tell her the truth about the engagement being fake and to be honest, the lines are so blurred now anyway that I'm not sure what's the truth and what's a lie.

'Is it Edward?' She sounds uncertain.

'Yes!' I force enthusiasm into my tone, 'Edward and I are getting married.'

'Wow! I didn't see that coming.' She pushes her chair back but I jump up from mine and go to her. 'Congratulations, Ava, darling. I'm happy for you.'

We hug for a bit then I go and sit back down and take my mug between my hands. The ring glints under the weak kitchen bulb, its sparkle duller in this room than anywhere in Edward's home. Reality sucks at my feet as it sinks in that I'm being dishonest here. And not just to Mum but to myself. This flat, this life, this kitchen... this is who I am and recently I've allowed myself to be carried along on a wave of contracts, Egyptian cotton sheets, organic fruit and veg, thick, creamy Greek yogurt and multiple orgasms supplied by my very own billionaire fiancé.

But he's not *my* billionaire. It's all a façade and being here makes that abundantly clear to me. I'm living a life that's not really mine to have, and it could all come crashing down around me. This is why I was afraid to come home sooner. I've been like a horse with blinkers on, ignoring what's going on outside of the bubble I've been existing in.

'Are you happy?' Mum asks, concern in her gaze.

'Yes, of course!' I look away, not wanting to crumble right here and now.

'Ava?'

I slowly look up and bite my lower lip to stop it wobbling.

'I'm sure that it's not all sunshine and roses being involved with a rich and powerful man and that life with him is very different from...' She gestures at the kitchen. 'What you're used to. But it doesn't mean that it can't work out. Where there's love, there's a way.'

'But... Dad.' I release the thought into the room like a bad smell. I hate talking about him with Mum because of the pain it brings to her eyes but I can't deny that his abandonment has affected us all. Despite everything, she's so strong and resilient and I hope that I am like her even if it's in a small way.

Mum sighs and rubs at her eyes. 'Not all men are like him.'

'How do you know when you can trust someone?'

'You don't.' She holds up her hands. 'It's a choice you have to make every day. However a relationship starts, there's no guarantee how it will end. You take each day as it comes and have faith that whatever happens, you've got your own back.'

At that moment, a sleepy Daniel walks into the kitchen and shrieks when he sees me. He flings himself into my arms and hugs me, smelling of sleep and fabric softener. He seems taller, his face changed, like he's grown up while I've been away, and I hug him tight. He's much bigger than Joe even though he's still just a boy. That thought makes me miss Joe, the child I've come to care about so deeply.

'Have you brought presents?' Daniel asks when he finally pulls away.

'Daniel! That's not nice to ask,' Mum scolds him but she's smiling.

'Of course I have. I've brought some for now and some for you to open on Christmas Day.'

'Won't you be here then?' He frowns.

'Not this year. But we'll make up for it next Christmas, I promise.'

'OK.' He grins with the easy joy of a child anticipating gifts in his near future.

If only it was as easy for an adult to enjoy the moment as it is for an innocent child.

Chapter 42

Ava

Five days after telling Mum that I'm engaged, I'm back in Buckinghamshire. I'd considered driving home – taking the car Edward gave me, but I was nervous about anything happening to it. We don't have a garage or even a driveway in Brixton so it would've been parked on the street and I knew I'd be checking on it at all hours of the day and night. Plus there's the parking permit hell that I didn't have the time or mind space to negotiate. It would have been far more stress than it was worth. I told Edward I'd take the train, but he insisted that Jeff drive me. And so Jeff picked me up and on the way he filled me in on how excited Joe was for Christmas and how the house was decorated and looking beautiful.

And it does. When I enter the hallway, I'm struck by how magnificent it is. A giant tree sits in the middle of the floor. It must be about seven foot tall and almost as wide. Polly will have arranged the decorations but I suspect that Edward was responsible for sourcing the tree. Small fairy lights twinkle in the afternoon gloom, peeping out from between the red and gold bows that have been tied to the branches. Lights and bunches of greenery adorn the banister all the way up and across the landing. There is a scent of pine and spice and it's then that I spot the bunches of cinnamon sticks and dried fruit in amongst the greenery and the bows on the tree.

'Hello, dear.' Polly appears and hugs me. 'We missed you.'

'I missed you too. It's very festive in here.'

'We do our best.'

'The smell is incredible.'

'Wait until you go in the kitchen. I've baked mince pies.'

'Yum!' I smile at her, my heart filled with fondness for this woman who has become both friend and mother figure. I have a feeling that she'll get on well with Mum and spoil Daniel as she does Joe. 'Are Joe and Edward here?'

'Joe's in the kitchen munching on a gingerbread star but Edward had to go to the office.'

'Oh, OK. I'll just take my bag up then I'll come and see Joe.'

Upstairs, I place my bag on the bed then go to the window. I had hoped to see Edward as soon as I got back so I'm a bit disappointed, but he probably has a lot to do this time of year. It'll be good to see Joe anyway, so I wash up then head on down to the kitchen.

In the hallway, I pause for a moment to admire the tree and a wave of sadness washes over me. In the flat, Mum had a small fake tree in the corner of the lounge that's got to be five years old at least. Some of the bulbs didn't work and the tinsel was thin and bitty. The best thing about the tree were the decorations that Dan and I had made over the years, the cottonwool ball snowmen, the cardboard angel, the small clay bell that Dan made in nursery school that has faded and become chipped over time but that still has his initials on the back. Things like that, the precious memories that we gather, matter more than any expensive decorations ever could. But even so, I went out and bought Mum and Daniel a new, bigger tree with built-in lights and some new decorations. I took Daniel with me and he chose them, his excitement brimming over at the approaching holiday. I also told Mum not to worry about looking for a place now because there's the possibility that we could all live together in Edward's house or she could get somewhere nearby for her and Daniel. I'd like them to live here but I don't want to put pressure on her and so I felt it was better to give her the options to consider. She said something about Daniel needing to finish the school year where he is, but I think she was just overwhelmed at the prospect of moving and living with people she's never met before. Which brings me back to something I need to speak to Edward about: when he's going to meet my Mum. He did offer before I went home but I told him that I needed to tell her myself first. Otherwise, I was worried it would be too much for her in one go.

In the kitchen, I find Joe at the table. He grins at me when I give him a hug and I have to swallow back tears because I'm so happy to see him.

'How're you doing?' I ask.

'I missed you, Ava. I was worried you wouldn't come back like my other mummy.'

I pull out a chair and sit near him while Polly busies herself at the stove.

Did he just refer to me as his mummy?

'Of course I'd come back. I just needed to visit my mum and brother.'

'Why didn't you take me with you?' His innocent question is like an arrow to my heart and I swallow hard.

'I had to go and see my family and you had school. But you're all done for the year now, so we can spend lots of time together over the holidays.'

'Will your brother be my friend?'

'I should think so. When you meet him, he can show you how good he is with Lego.'

Joe smiles and I could squish him up and never let go. Instead, I settle for leaning over and kissing his hair. The scent of his shampoo makes my ovaries jump, I swear.

'Can I come next time?' he asks.

'I should think so. Or, even better, my mum and brother can come here.'

He nods. 'Have a gingerbread star, Ava. I made them with Polly and I did the icing.'

'Oooh, yes please.'

And while I nibble on gingerbread, Joe tells me all about his last few days at school and the concert they put on for the parents. I was sad to miss it but I did need to get home while I could.

'Daddy filmed it for you on his phone so you can watch it later with me.' Joe smiles and I smooth his hair back from his forehead.

'I'll look forward to it,' I say.

He taps the ring on my left hand. 'You're going to be my mummy now, aren't you?'

'Edward has explained to him that you'll be his wife and so that means you'll also be Joe's mummy,' Polly says.

'Right.' I nod. I wasn't sure how Edward would tell Joe but I kind of thought we might do it together. However, this is good too because Joe has had some time to get used to it.

'Now we'll always be together.' Joe slides off his chair

and gives me a hug and as I rest my head on his shoulder, I think *I hope so*, because leaving him now would be unbearable. I can't even bear to think ahead to how it will feel when our marriage of convenience comes to an end, as I assume it will do at some point.

Chapter 43

Edward

I rushed back from London last night, knowing that Ava would be at home, but I was too late and she was already in bed. It was probably a good thing because even though she'd only been gone a few days, I've missed her and I might have behaved irresponsibly. And yes, by that I mean, taking her to bed. I can't get enough of her sweetness, how she threads her hands though my hair and presses me into her, whispering my name as she climaxes. I've held back from penetrating her or letting her pleasure me because I'm afraid of losing control. Not physically, because it's not the act itself but what it represents and what it could do to her. It could deepen whatever it is that's going on between us and I don't want her to get hurt. Plus, though I hate to admit it, for me it's been over two years and I can't bear the thought of losing myself to another woman. I can't afford to be hurt like that again. But I can give Ava pleasure and I enjoy doing it. It's something that I can offer her without completely surrendering myself. And she tastes so fucking good that I can't get enough of her.

This evening we have a Christmas party at one of the

neighbouring estates. I've known the family all my life. Joe will stay with Polly but Ava will come with me and then I can publicly share that we plan to marry in the new year, although the unofficial news has been out since Halloween.

The final draft of the contract is ready for Ava to sign and then we'll be all systems go. While she was away, the house felt empty without her. Joe was a bit lost and I know I was too. Ava brings something with her and the only way I can describe it is that she's like a ray of sunshine on a cloudy day. She brings warmth and joy that the house has been missing and the fact that she's agreed to sign a contract that will keep her here for the foreseeable future offers me more relief than I can articulate.

Soon, Ava Thorne will be my bride. That day can't come soon enough.

Chapter 44

Ava

Edward drives us to the Christmas Eve party in his sleek, silver Aston Martin. The car is gorgeous and I sit back, watching the road ahead glowing in the moonlight as he drives through the country lanes, the frosty hedgerows and fields flying past in a blur. I catch him glancing at me several times and I wish I knew what he was thinking because he's been quiet since this morning when I saw him at breakfast.

I'm wearing a short red-lace dress that I found on my bed after lunch, sent direct from a designer I suspect, and it's risen up my legs in the low car seat. Underneath the dress I have on black holdup stockings and a lacy black thong that was provided with the dress. The thong is soft against my skin, teasing me where it touches. There was no bra so I'm not wearing one and with the low back of the dress, I didn't have a suitable one anyway. On my feet are glittery black Manolo Blahniks that I keep admiring. They're so pretty and sparkly and make my legs look far longer than they are. Along with the shoes was a clutch and in that I've put my phone and lip-gloss. Edward also arranged for the hairstylist and makeup artist to come again so I certainly look the part of the billionaire's fiancée this evening.

I tug at the dress and try to pull it down but every time I move, it slides up again.

'Stop fidgeting,' he says, his eyes on my legs. Something rebellious kicks in. I've missed being close to him, feeling his hands on me. His sultry cologne is teasing my senses, making me want him, so I deliberately wriggle causing the dress to ride up and expose the lacy tops of the stockings.

His breath catches in his throat, and I bite my lip to hide my smile, but then his hand is on my thigh and my core clenches. He moves his hand higher, brushes it over the front of the flimsy thong and I can't help myself, I moan. I've never been like this, so wanton, so alive, but Edward has this effect on me and I'm sure it's because my feelings for him are far deeper than anything I've experienced before. No man has ever touched me the way he does and I want him constantly.

'You like that?' His voice is low, guttural.

'Yes,' I whisper.

'More later,' he says, flashing me a grin, and I could cry with frustration.

He removes his hand and gives my thigh a squeeze then manoeuvrers the car up a long, winding driveway. He pulls up outside a large, three storey blond stone Georgian mansion with a panelled door framed by two large columns. The front of the house is illuminated with exterior lighting that draws attention to the parapet and sash windows and I'm sure I've seen it in a Jane Austen adaptation.

Edward gets out then comes around to the passenger side and offers me his hand. I try to get out gracefully but in the short dress and heels, it's hard, and as I stand, I lose my balance and fall towards Edward. He catches me and for a moment, I lean against him, feeling his strong hands around my waist, his hard body pressed against mine. He gives my bottom a quick squeeze and it's all I can do not to press my hand to his crotch.

'Good evening, Sir and Madam.' I step back as a man in a dark suit appears at Edward's side. Edward drops the car keys into the man's open palm.

'Shall we?' Edward holds out his arm and I take it then we climb the steps to the front door.

I glance behind me to see that other cars are pulling up in front of the house and the man who took Edward's keys gets into the Aston Martin and drives it away. It's like something out of an awards ceremony and again reminds me what a different life Edward leads.

The front door of the house opens revealing a giant Christmas tree with sparkling lights and another man in a black suit smiles at us then ushers us inside. My stomach flips over because I'm suddenly nervous about meeting these people who Edward has known since childhood. What if they look down on me and think I'm out of place?

'Don't worry,' Edward says softly. 'You'll be brilliant.'

And then we are immersed in welcomes and air kisses, and I hold on tight to my fiancé's arm as he works the room. He's so sophisticated and clearly well thought of by his peers. He shakes hands and kisses cheeks as he greets people, introducing me to everyone without fail and soon I give up trying to remember the names. Most of the people I meet seem friendly enough, to be fair, and I only receive a few cold glances. By now, I'm sure it's out that I'm the nanny but Edward's confidence rubs off on me and so I raise my chin and smile as if I have no idea that anyone could be questioning my right to be there.

When Edward introduces me to the owners of the stately home, I smile at them. Timothy Seymour is a tall man in his sixties with a large belly and red cheeks and he greets me with genuine warmth. His wife, Ellen, smiles but her mouth seems pinched, as if she's being polite but would really rather that I wasn't gracing her home with my working-class presence. Edward asks after their children Dempsey, Spencer and Margot, making me wonder if they have a book of names suitable for showing off their wealth and status.

And then we move on, and Edward leads me to a quiet corner. He grabs a champagne flute from a passing tray and presses it into my hand.

'Drink,' he says and I do, gratefully imbibing the cold, crisp drink. 'Are you OK?'

'I think so.' I nod and take another sip of champagne. 'So many names I'm dizzy. I'll never remember them all.'

'You don't need to.' He shakes his head. 'We'll only see the majority of them at Christmas and we can do some revision before next year.' His wink makes me giggle.

He sounds so certain, reminding me that we'll be together for a while and it's both reassuring and yet terrifying. Right now, Edward is being kind and attentive because he still wants something from me but will that change when I sign the marriage contract? Will having my commitment turn him off me the way that my mum's love and devotion to my father failed to keep him close?

'What's wrong?' he asks.

'Nothing.' I drain my glass and he takes it and places it on an ornate side table.

'Come with me.' He takes my hand and leads me through the house, away from the chatter and the waiting staff. After looking around, he pushes a door then pulls me through and closes it behind us.

The smell of books hits me first followed by a faint whiff of woodsmoke and something else that I think is beeswax furniture polish. I crane my neck to look beyond Edward but he has me pinned against the door.

His chest is rising and falling quickly and there's something in his eyes that makes me nervous. His Adam's apple bobs and he licks his lips hungrily.

'What is it?' I ask.

'It's you.' He rubs his eyes. 'In this damned dress. I knew you'd look good in it but fuck, Ava, you're so hot that I can barely keep my hands to myself.'

I don't know what to say to this because my desire for him is a physical ache.

'I'm sorry,' he says.

'Why are you sorry?'

'I'm struggling.' He steps away and paces the room, creating space between us and I feel cold, want him close to me again. The room is lit by table lamps, bright enough to see but dark enough to create shadows in the corners and it makes me suddenly irrationally afraid that the darkness could encroach upon us and swallow us whole.

'Tell me.' I push away from the door and approach him but he holds up a hand.

'This is a business arrangement and I thought I could do it without getting involved with you, but...'

'It's hard, right?' I ask and he meets my eyes.

'So hard.'

I hold out a hand and he looks at it, a muscle in his jaw twitching. And then he comes to me, quickly, and I'm against the door again, the panels digging into my shoulder blades. His lips are close to mine, so close I can feel the heat of his breath.

'You're driving me crazy, Ava. I've been shut down for so long and now, you're doing something to me that I don't understand.'

He moves closer and kisses me gently, feathering his lips over my mouth, my neck and then lower. He slides the dress off my shoulders and exposes my breasts, takes them in his hands, squeezing, cupping, adoring. When he lowers his head and takes my right nipple in his mouth, I arch my back to give him better access and he suckles at me, his hunger making something at my core tighten like there's a link from nipple to pussy. He moves to the other breast and I grab his head, pressing him closer, wanting more.

'You're fucking gorgeous,' he mutters before filling his mouth with me again.

'I want you so much,' I say and he looks up, all rational thought gone from his eyes, something far more primal there now.

He hitches up my dress, pushes the thong aside then slides a finger over my clit, up and down, building tension inside me. I open my legs wider to give him better access and he pushes a finger inside me then another while he circles my clit with the pad of his thumb. Within seconds an orgasm crashes through me and I bite down on my lip to stop myself crying out.

'You're soaking wet, Ava,' he says, holding up his hand to show me. He licks his fingers slowly, the action reminding me of how good that tongue feels between my legs. 'And you taste like champagne.'

'Make love to me, Edward.'

He pauses for a moment then takes my hand and places

it on his crotch. Beneath his suit trousers he's rock hard and I want him inside me, filling me up and making me whole.

'I can't,' he says. 'I don't have anything with me.'

'I don't care.'

He shakes his head but unzips his trousers and pulls out his cock. It's big and hard and I can only imagine how it would feel thrusting into me. Edward places my hand on the shaft but I drop to my knees and take him between my lips. I lick the tip, tasting him, cup his balls with my hand and grip his tight ass with the other. I have to relax my jaw to accommodate him but when he slides his fingers into my hair and drives his length into me, I know I'm pleasing him.

His thrusting speeds up, his cock seems to swell and suddenly he takes a step back as if to pull out of me, but I move with him. I keep sucking him until he cries out my name then I swallow every last drop, hold him in my mouth until he is spent.

He pulls me to stand with him, gently slides my dress down over my thighs and kisses my breasts before pulling the bodice of my dress over them. I am so weak that if he wasn't right in front of me, holding me up, I would sink to the floor.

'What are you doing to me, woman?' he asks before kissing me so tenderly that my heart sings.

When we get home after the party, I remove my shoes in the downstairs hallway then climb the stairs. I check on Joe and find him sleeping cuddled up to a teddy bear. I tuck the covers around him and kiss his forehead. When I look up, Edward is watching me from the adjoining doorway. He crosses the room and kisses Joe then leads me out to the hallway and walks me to my room.

'Joe will be up early,' he says. 'It's probably better if we sleep in our own rooms. Besides which, I have to help Santa.'

'Do you want a hand?' Having done this for Daniel, I know it can be fun but also time consuming.

'It's fine,' he says. 'Jeff's already getting everything in from the garage and I'll just add the final touches.'

It must be great to have staff to help with things like that. I can remember Mum hiding gifts behind her clothes in the wardrobe and even asking one of the neighbours to have the second-hand bike she bought Daniel one year in their shed until Christmas Eve.

'Of course.' I know he's being sensible but I feel spurned, as if he doesn't want me now. I'd like to help but I also don't want to overstep any lines in case Edward doesn't want me to. I also don't think that Joe would care if he found us in bed together tomorrow but it's a risk and the last thing I want is to hurt him. Edward is his father and so he knows best; it is his decision to make.

'Goodnight, Ava,' Edward says, caressing my cheek before placing a warm kiss on my lips.

I watch as he crosses the landing and descends the stairs then go into my room and close the door, yawning as exhaustion claims me. Tomorrow will be busy so sleep will do me good.

As I slip between the cool covers, I lie back and let the events of the evening play through my mind and soon I drift into sleep where Edward once again graces my dreams.

Chapter 45

Ava

'Ava! Wake up!'

I do, to the sensation of someone tapping my face. Blinking, I peer through the mess of my hair at Joe.

'It's Christmas Day! Come on, we need to see if Father Christmas has been.'

He bounces on the spot and so I shake my head to clear the sleep fog then peer through the grey light. 'What time is it?'

'Just after five,' Edward says from the doorway. 'I told you he'd be up early this morning.'

'Oh god,' I say as I push back the covers and swing my legs over the side of the bed. 'Let me just grab my robe.'

When we descend the stairs, Joe between us, the smell of pine and spice greets me and I breathe it in, savouring the festive smell. The tree lights and those on the banisters twinkle in the gloom. It's like a Christmas advert on TV and I'm actually inside it!

We go to the main lounge and there, in front of the tree

in the corner of the room, is a pile of colourfully wrapped gifts.

'Wow!' It's a big pile.

'Father Christmas has been!' Joe claps his hands. 'Can I open them, Daddy?'

'Of course,' Edward says.

We sit side by side on the sofa while Joe tears through paper. A fire, already lit before I got up, crackles in the grate and outside, light starts to brighten the sky. When Polly comes in with a tray of coffee, I accept a mug gratefully, and cradle it between my hands.

Joe has some lovely gifts and it makes me think of Daniel. Has he got up yet? Is Mum OK? I'll message them after breakfast to say Merry Christmas.

'This is for you,' Edward says, interrupting my thoughts.

'You got me something?' I ask.

'Of course.'

'Thank you so much.' I accept the gift, untie the ribbon then lift off the lid. Inside is a beautiful diamond bracelet. 'Goodness.'

'Let me put it on.' Edward fastens it around my left wrist and I realise that along with the engagement ring, I'm wearing a small fortune.

'It's beautiful. I don't know if I'll ever get used to this.'

'You will.' He smiles. 'In time.'

'I got Joe some things but they're upstairs so I'll get them when he's finished there. Also, I got you something too,' I say, reaching into the deep pocket of my fleecy robe. It took some thought to find this gift because, well, what do you get a billionaire?

He unwraps the gift and smiles. 'Cufflinks.'

'They're solid silver collectibles. I didn't know what to get you.'

'Who are the people?' he asks with a frown, looking at the silhouettes on each cufflink.

'It's Cinderella and Prince Charming,' I say, surprised he didn't know.

'I love them.' He smiles. 'Are you saying that I'm your Prince Charming?'

'Something like that. Except Prince Charming didn't already have a child and Cinderella didn't come from a council flat in Brixton. Plus, as far as I know, he didn't ask her to sign a contract or pay her.' The words are out before I can stop them, and I mean it as a joke but Edward winces. 'Edward... I'm sorry. I meant it in jest but yes, you are like a prince to me. This whole lifestyle is so different to the life I had and I am grateful to you. In more ways than one you've changed my life.'

And I mean it. The money will offer freedom I never had before but it's so much more than that. I have feelings for this man and for his son, feelings I can't deny to myself. I have no idea how to deal with them because I've never felt like this before. I'm scared but I'm also excited but I don't know how to say all this to him.

'You've changed my life too, Ava,' he says softly.

Before I can respond, he stands and goes to Joe. 'Time for some breakfast, champ. You can play with all of this later.'

We go to the kitchen but Polly shakes her head and tells us to go to the dining room. It's rarely been used during my time here but Polly did tell me Edward and Lucille used it when they entertained. The kitchen is far more homely than the airy room with its long, rectangular table, but it is Christmas so I guess this makes sense.

The fire blazing in the grate makes the room more appealing and we sit at one end of the table together. There are five places and I'm delighted when Polly and Jeff join us. Our own little group together for Christmas.

Breakfast is a delicious buffet of smoked salmon, scrambled eggs and English muffins spread with thick, golden butter. To wash it down, we drink Bellinis and I feel pleasantly tipsy.

Sitting back, I look around the table and my chest swells with affection for these people. Four months ago, I didn't know any of them, but in that time they've become like family and I'm so grateful to have them in my life.

Chapter 46

Edward

Christmas Day is a celebration of good food, excellent company and of being alive. Ava's presence makes it so much better than in recent years and I enjoy having her around. She brings a sense of joy and hope with her and the shadow I've lived under for so long is lifting. It hasn't gone completely but neither is it there all the time anymore. It makes me realise that I don't like the idea of her not being here. The marriage contract will bind us together legally but this is growing into more than just a legal obligation and that is both heart-warming and terrifying.

What if Ava decides she wants out at some point?

What if she decides to leave? I'll manage, of course I will, but what about Joe? He's lost one mother and losing another will be too much for him, surely?

I loved Lucille but we were young when we got together and I was naïve. What happened between us taught me that you can't ever really know someone. You'll never be aware of what's going on in their heart or their mind and what if Ava is not who she seems to be? People can deceive others.

It's possible that she's only here for the money. Shit, I know she's here for the money because this all started with her coming here to work for me but now there's a lot more on the table for her. Time is running out for me to find someone else and so I know that we need to follow this through and yet... Part of me is scared that she'll cut and run at some point in the future. I've been fooled once and I don't want to be fooled again.

I need to pull back, to be master of my emotions and not some gullible romantic. I'm paying Ava for her time and she'll get plenty out of our deal so I'll take what I want but keep my distance emotionally.

And yet... as I watch her playing with Joe, as I catch her glancing at me and smiling, I find it so difficult to believe that she's at all disingenuous. How could one person pretend to be so lovely? Surely it's impossible?

Or is she simply too good to be true?

Chapter 47

Ava

Joe is tucked up in bed. It was a busy but wonderful day and now Edward and I are in the lounge. The fire creates a warm, cosy glow and we're sitting at opposite ends of the sofa cracking nuts and drinking mulled wine. Outside, snow is falling and the land beyond the window is pure white, lit by the moon that sits high above the house. After we'd tucked Joe in, I gazed out of the bedroom window for ages, unable to tear my eyes away from the beauty of the estate. There is so much space here and it allows me to breathe, something I never had at the flat. Edward and Joe are in my heart now but this place, this land, this home is too. I feel like I belong here and that is scary because I know that this could end once I've met the terms of the marriage contract. Edward said that we will have to stay together for at least a year after the spring wedding and I wanted to ask, *What then? Will I be asked to leave?*

Polly and Jeff have retired for the night and so it's just Edward and me. He has Christmas songs playing on the Bluetooth speaker and I am completely relaxed. It's easy to pretend that this is my life and we'll see in the new year as a real couple, will marry for love in the spring.

'I have something else for you, Ava,' Edward says, sitting upright.

'You do?' I push myself to the edge of the enormous, squishy sofa and take another sip of warm, spiced wine.

'Hold on.' He gets up and leaves the room then returns with an A4 envelope that he hands to me.

'What is it?' I ask, although I already know as I peel back the seal and reach inside. It's the marriage contract.

'You don't need to read it now but I wanted you to have it so we both know where we stand going forwards,' he says, not meeting my eyes.

'Edward... I...' There are things I want to say and yet I'm not sure how to vocalise them. 'This is necessary, I know that, and yet it's... so formal.'

'You signed a contract before,' he says.

'That was different. It was for a job.'

'This is a job,' he replies. His tone is slightly off, as if he's put his business hat on and it saddens me. I don't want it to be like this between us. He sways sometimes from being the man I adore to a hard-headed businessman and it knocks me off balance. I don't know how he can be two such different people, although I do suspect that he uses the businessman to protect himself like a suit of armour. I wish I knew what it is that he's so scared of. He lost Lucille, I know that, but she didn't choose to leave him. We've had such a lovely day. I've never spent Christmas with a man before and Edward has been the perfect companion. We've had fun, laughed lots, eaten too much food and I felt like we were a family.

Placing the contract and the envelope on the coffee table, I shuffle closer to him.

'Edward... just for tonight can we be two people who like each other?'

'What do you mean?' He eyes me warily.

'Can we be Edward and Ava, not people conducting a business transaction. I know you're my employer but can all that wait until tomorrow?' Perhaps it's the wine or because it's Christmas but I feel brave and I want to act on it.

I stroke the side of his face and he shivers before turning to me. 'Ava... I don't want to hurt you.'

'You won't,' I say with surety, ignoring the tiny voice at the back of my mind telling me to take care.

His chest rises and falls, rises and falls then he seems to make a decision. He takes my wrist and pulls me onto his lap, squeezing my behind hard enough to make me jump. Before I know what's happening, his mouth is on mine and his one hand roams over my breasts while the other winds itself in my hair, holding me in place. I am caught, held fast, and I like it. No one has ever made me feel this way and I am glad. I want it to be another first with Edward, to be possessed by him and to possess him right back.

When he pulls away, I groan but he says, 'Are you sure? I don't want to take advantage of you.'

'I'm sure.'

'Say it.'

'I want you, Edward. I want you inside me.'

His eyes are dark pools of desire and when he stands and drags his jumper over his head, I gasp at his beauty. His chest is sculpted, his arms muscular, his abs defined. His trousers hang low on his hips and I admire the fine muscles that lead down to his groin. He pushes the trousers down and his thick cock bobs free, already hard.

For me.

He wants me too.

I lie back and ease my trousers down but he's on top of me before I can remove my jumper, pushing it up to my chin and feathering kisses all over my breasts. He squeezes my nipples hard, rolls them between thumb and fingertip, creating that delicious jolt of sensation between nipple and womb, then he reaches down and slides his fingers inside me.

'Wet already.' He emits a low growl. 'Wet for me.'

When he kisses lower and his tongue finds my clit, I raise my hips as he sucks at the aroused nub, rotating his fingers inside me until I cry out with sheer ecstasy. I pulsate onto his fingers and he licks slowly at my clit until the climax wanes.

'Come inside me now.'

'I don't have a condom.'

'Upstairs?'

He nods and we grab our clothes and dash across the hall, the moonlight shining through the window above the front door illuminating our naked white flesh like a spotlight.

Upstairs, he pulls me inside his room and shuts the door behind us then places a finger over his lips. Joe is sleeping next door, so of course we need to be quiet.

I climb onto his bed and lie back, waiting for him. Anticipating how it will feel to finally hold him inside me.

Soon he's with me again, panting and laughing at the madness of it all. He kisses me harder now, and I taste the wine on his lips, shiver as he moves over me and rests on his elbows. He rubs the tip of his cock against my folds, opening me to him, finding his way home. When he finally pushes inside me, I hold his gaze, wanting our connection in every way at this longed-for moment. He lies still for a few seconds as I adjust my hips to take him deeper then he starts to move.

My desire rises again and soon I'm grabbing his hips and pushing him into me as hard as I can. My orgasm crashes over me before I'm aware that it's coming, and stars rush before my eyes. I bite his shoulder to stop myself screaming with pleasure. He comes soon after me, shuddering as he holds me tight; warm, sated and still connected to me.

Eventually, he rolls over, tidies himself up then lies on his back and I snuggle into his chest. As I drift off in my post coital glow, I know that I could easily fall deeply in love with this man. The question is, does he feel the same?

The question is, am I able to let go of my past in order to love him in the way he deserves?

Chapter 48

Ava

When I wake, I reach out for Edward, but he's gone, leaving just the slight imprint of his body on the mattress. It takes me a few minutes to come around properly and as I do, several things hit me.

We slept together.

I felt something deeper than desire.

Have we made an enormous mistake?

I get up and in the grey light seeping around the edge of the curtains, I search for my clothes and dress quickly. The room is cold but it barely registers with me because of the chill in my heart. I have given myself to this man and he has left me.

Men always leave...

The voice comes from nowhere and I look around as if expecting to see someone sitting on the chair in the corner. Goosebumps rise on my arms and it hits me like a ton of bricks. This is the room Edward shared with Lucille. They spent many nights here together and this must be difficult for Edward. He loved Lucille, they had a child together and then he lost her. Moving on from that must be incredibly difficult, whatever it is he's feeling for me it won't be a fraction of what he felt for her. They had a real marriage; we will not.

There are too many ghosts in this house, the attic is full of them in the form of photographs, videos and his wife's belongings. How can I compete with a ghost? Surely that's impossible?

Edward is vulnerable and still, in many ways, broken. He needs to continue his healing journey and being with me might not help with that. I have my own demons and so, as much as I wish I could be with him, I'm not capable of helping him to banish his.

As for me... I'm tangled in a web of conflicting feelings. I never thought I'd care about a man like this. I never believed I'd get married after seeing how much my father hurt my mum. But here I am, falling for my boss *and* we're engaged. Edward might think he wants this but is it the right move for him to make? We come from different social classes. I'm his child's nanny, for crying out loud. *The nanny!* How will I ever compare to Lucille the model, the first wife and mother? I'll spend my days walking in her shadow, never meeting her standards, never making Edward happy because he'll always wish I was her.

I can't live like this because it will break me apart. I know I could make significant life changes if I married him but there's too much at stake.

My heart.

My sanity.

My life.

I can make things better for Mum and Daniel with what

I've made already from being a nanny so I'll see out the job contract then leave.

After last night, I know for certain that I am in love with Edward, and therefore, I cannot be his fake wife. I have to be true to myself and to my feelings.

I have to let him go.

Chapter 49

Edward

I am a coward. A fucking coward.

My breath emerges like puffs of smoke as I tramp through the woods on the estate. It is freezing on this first day of the year but it's nothing compared to the chill in my bones, the ice around my shattered heart.

I slept with Ava on Christmas night. I took her beautiful body in my arms and made love to her. It was incredible. But it also brought emotions to the surface that I thought I'd buried with Lucille. And so, after we'd made love, I crept out of bed while Ava slept and went to my study, sought solace in my business as I have done for years.

Christmas Day was one of the best days I've ever had, but that terrified me. I gave myself to Lucille, I trusted in what we had and I loved her and look what happened. After I lost her, I swore I'd never care about someone else or give my heart again, but bit by bit, day by day, Ava has got under my skin and I knew that making love to her would be dangerous. I thought, hoped, that I could separate the physical act from my emotions but as soon as I held her in my arms and entered her perfect, warm and soft body, felt her contract around me, everything changed.

I cannot let myself love her.

So what did I do?

I distanced myself from her. I left early on Boxing Day and went to London, to the apartment I keep there and I buried myself in work. I messaged her to let her know that something had come up and asked her to tell Joe. I returned to the estate two days later to spend time with Joe, but I kept my distance from Ava and she seemed happy to do the same.

Today is the official end of her contract as Joe's nanny and she hasn't signed the marriage contract so I have no idea what's going to happen. I want to go to her and ask her to sign it so I know what comes next but that would mean seeing her feelings in her eyes and I just can't be that close to her. It also makes me feel like the worst kind of bastard because I slept with her then I turned my back on her. I still need her to marry me but I also don't know if I can put her through that. It's all such a mess and it was meant to be straightforward, uncomplicated, a way to avoid drama.

But sleeping with her confirmed for me that if we do marry, it can only be a marriage of convenience and not a love match. Business deals work for me because I keep my heart out of them. In love, I am a failure, but in business I am in control, hard hearted and focused. It's my safe place and so this must be about business and nothing more.

I will give Ava wealth beyond her dreams, a home and my name, but I cannot, will not, give her my heart.

Chapter 50

Ava

Life can change in an instant.
The mind and heart don't always agree.
I have gone with my mind. Or is it my heart?
Sitting in the small kitchen with cooking stains up the wall behind the hob that won't come off however hard I scrub them, whatever miracle stain remover I use, I sip my supermarket brand instant coffee and try to remain calm. The clock ticks. The tap drips. A crow squawks outside on the windowsill, fluffing up its feathers against the freezing January air. I am Cinderella the day after the ball, thrust back to the hearth and the ashes of her dreams. I left everything from my life with Edward behind, except for the book necklace that Joe gave me and that is around my neck, close to my heart.

I swipe at my cheeks, brushing away the tears that keep flowing, because I made a decision and now I have to live with the consequences. Adulting isn't easy and no one ever claimed that it would be.

Much has changed since August. My bank account is full. My debts paid off. The laptop on the table in front of me is top of the range. It is open to a webpage of properties I want Mum to consider as potential new homes. Life always moves on. Whatever happens; illness, death, heartbreak, it keeps going. I will survive this and one day, my time with Edward and Joe will feel like a dream. A beautiful, confusing dream. It already feels surreal, like I imagined it. After all, how could one man be so wonderful? How could I grow to care for him and his child so deeply?

I could have signed the marriage contract. I could have pretended in order to live in luxury, to stay near to Edward and near to Joe. Believe me, it was a struggle of epic proportions to turn away from the little boy, but in the end, I had to be true to myself.

I love Edward.

I love Joe.

That means that I cannot live a lie. I cannot be near Edward every day and know that he doesn't love me. It would be torture and I am not strong enough for that. If I could be cold and hard then perhaps I would manage it, but over time I believe it would wear me down. I saw what loving a man who kept walking away did to my mum and I will not live that life myself. She kept believing in my father, kept hoping he'd change and every time he walked back in, she'd think that this would be the time he stayed. The last time, when she was ill, she believed he meant it when he said he loved her and then, one night, he was gone. Her purse was cleared out, her meagre jewellery box too, but the worst thing of all was how he had shattered her heart. And so, here I am, back where I started.

Part of me feels bad for Edward and Joe. A big part, in fact. I would have been able to secure the inheritance of majority shares and the role of CEO for Edward by marrying him and I did consider it, especially after

Christmas Day. But it would have meant surrendering a large part of who I am and that would not have been fair on Mum and Daniel, and neither would it have been fair on me. We get one life: it's not a rehearsal. I want to be me. I want to be the woman I was raised to be. I am not capable of being fake. Being close to Edward would have broken me with time. So much love cannot be buried, hidden away in a spare room like old furniture, gathering dust. Love needs the light, it needs to be nurtured, to evolve and to grow. If we try to curb it in any way, it can drive us mad and I am not prepared to be the mad woman locked away in the attic — albeit it metaphorically.

So here I am. Home. Where I belong.

Cynthia was back before I left and Joe was delighted to see her so I know he'll be OK. Edward too. I'm sure Edward will find another woman to marry him so he can keep the estate and hopefully she'll be strong enough to accept that he can't give her love.

'Morning, Ava.' Mum shuffles into the kitchen wearing the fluffy red dressing gown I bought her for Christmas and the new soft wool moccasin slippers that are nice and roomy for when her feet swell.

'Hey, Mum.' I get up and we hug, and I bite the inside of my cheek to stop emotion overwhelming me. 'Coffee?' I ask, turning away so she won't see the pain on my face.

'That would be lovely.' She sinks into a chair and I make coffee then place it in front of her.

She looks at me in the way that tells me that I'm fooling no one, but she doesn't say anything. When I got home, she had a thousand questions and I told her I'd explain in time. But for now, I need to get through the days and heal, create the life for her and Daniel that I've always wanted to give them.

'What are our plans today?' she asks once she's drunk her coffee.

I slide the laptop in front of her.

'I thought we could do some online house hunting.'

The smile that spreads over her face warms me right through.

She takes my hand and holds on tight, and I know that while my heart is broken, I have done the right thing for us all.

Chapter 51

Edward

'You're walking around like a zombie,' Polly's voice jerks me upright. I grab my mug of coffee and take it to the kitchen table.

I had no idea I could miss someone so much. Yes, I missed Lucille but me memories of her were tarnished by what I'd found out and this is different in so many ways. Ava is still alive, out there walking around in the world and I'm not with her. It's all my fault. I brought this on me and Joe. It's killing me. Seriously, this pain is unbearable. Everything I've been through over the years should have toughened me up but losing Ava has rocked me.

'What?' My tone is sharper than I intended. 'I mean, pardon?'

'Edward, love, I've worked for your family for a long time, and I know you've had a difficult few years but... There's no easy way to say this so I'm just going to get it out.' She places her hands on the back of a chair and sighs. 'This is your fault.'

'What do you mean?' I pinch the bridge of my nose hard. I like Polly but she's treading a fine line here.

'You could have persuaded Ava to stay.'

'You think so?' Now my tone sounds desperate.

'Yes.' She nods. 'That young woman adores you and Joe. Plus, she was like a breath of fresh air around the place and she made such a difference to us all.'

'You too, huh?'

'Yes. Me too. I care about you and Joe, but I also care about Ava. She has a good heart and she fitted in here. It's not that I didn't like Miss Lucille, because she was a... very glamorous lady, but Ava is... different.'

'You can say that again.' I give a small laugh but then rub my hands over my face, feeling the scratch as they move over my untended beard.

'Different can be a good thing, Edward. Ava brought something to this house that we needed. She brought you back to life. She was a tonic for Joe. She would have been good for you if you'd allowed her in.'

Meeting Polly's wise eyes, I nod. She's only telling me what I already know. It's been three weeks since Ava left, and every day has been agony. Joe is back at school but I see how much he misses her. Cynthia is home and she's doing her best for him but he's gone quiet again and lacks the enthusiasm for things that he had when Ava was here. I did this to him by being so pig headed, by not grabbing hold of Ava and making her feel loved. I wanted to prove to her that she's special but then I let fear get in the way.

What kind of idiot am I?

'Edward... you get one life and if you want to spend yours with Ava... I'm sure it's not too late.'

I swallow my coffee in one gulp then push the chair back. When Ava went, she left the engagement ring, bracelet and necklace I bought her on the bed with a note apologising for letting me down with the marriage contract.

Seeing that she hadn't taken them with her was like a spear to my gut. It was a rejection of all we'd had together and it made me realise exactly how much she was going through. Ava was never bothered about my money, about anything other than true feelings. She needed the job, of course she did, but the rest of it meant nothing to her without love. How many women like that are actually out there? I'll never find someone else like her, someone who gets me and wants to be with me *for* me.

I'll never find another Ava.

'You're right, Polly. I must at least try to get her back.'

I just need to figure out how…

Chapter 52

Ava

'I'm excited to see this property,' I say to Mum as we walk up the driveway. The house is semi-detached with a small front garden and on a quiet street in Croydon. But the closer we get, the worse it looks. Having never house hunted before, I've been finding it more challenging to find something suitable than I'd realised. We'll have to leave London for sure, and we don't mind, but I had hoped to find us a property that we could move straight into. Instead, there are lots requiring significant renovations to make them habitable.

'Hmmm.' Mum nods but her lips are pressed together and I know she's reserving judgement until we've seen the inside.

Daniel is at school and it's a good thing or he'd have been horrified at some of the properties we've viewed.

The agent turns back to us at the front door and holds up the key. 'Perhaps I should let you go and take a look. The property has been vacant for some time and if you go in alone, you can have a good browse around and get a feel for the place. It has plenty of potential.'

'Oh... OK.' I accept the key and push it into the lock then stand back to let Mum in before me.

The hallway smells musty and the floor is bare apart from a thick covering of dust. The staircase is to the right, the lounge to the left and the kitchen is straight ahead. We glance into the lounge that seems to be stuck in the 1970s with bold yellow and brown wallpaper and an orange carpet that has brighter patches where the furniture must have been.

I try to do what I've seen on the property programmes we've watched recently and to imagine the house as a blank canvas. But it's tough. The smell and the colours are making my head hurt. We go back to the hall and then to the kitchen. This house is small but I'd grown used to Edward's grand mansion and so anything would seem small in comparison.

Don't think about him!

I take a deep, ragged breath then regret it as the smell of the house fills my nostrils. Coughing, I follow Mum to the kitchen and notice that the back door is open. The previous viewer must have left it unlocked unless it was the estate agent trying to air the place.

As I peer outside, I notice that there's someone in the garden. A tall man in a black suit, gazing at something beyond the fence at the end. He must be checking the property out too. But there is something familiar about the set of his shoulders in the dark jacket, the cut of his hair, the...

He turns around and I scream.

'Ava? What is it?' Mum asks.

My hand is over my mouth and I'm shaking my head.

'It can't be,' I mutter against my palm.

Mum places a hand on my shoulder and looks out of the door.

'Who's that?' She frowns then pulls her glasses from her bag and puts them on. 'Isn't that your boss? I mean, *former* boss? Edward Cavendish?'

My head bobs as he walks slowly up the garden and my heart is beating so hard I feel like I'm going to pass out.

'Go and say hello.' Mum nudges me so I glance at her.

'Why are you so calm?'

She smiles and then I realise. She knew he would be here. In this run-down property where he is incongruous in his expensive suit with his crisp white shirt and shiny shoes. Edward would never buy a place like this. So what's he doing here?

'Go on, love.' She pats my back. 'I'll wait out the front with the estate agent. I can't stay in here because the smell is awful.'

'OK.' I nod. 'Mum?'

'Yes, love.'

'I'm scared.'

'Don't be scared, Ava. Grab hold of happiness with both hands. That man has things he needs to say so give him a chance. That's all he wants.'

'You've spoken to him?'

'Mum's the word.' She winks at me then walks back through the house and I'm left alone, standing in the doorway, on pause between my past and my future, wondering what to do next.

Chapter 53

Ava

Thirty minutes later, we're settled in a small pub a short drive away from the property. Mum is in the bar, having lunch with Jeff — who drove us here — and Edward and I are alone. We have glasses of rich, ruby wine and he has offered me lunch too, but I can barely swallow the wine let alone eat.

'It's good to see you,' he says, running his finger along the base of his glass.

'You too.' I take a sip of wine, hoping it will wash down the lump of emotion that's lodged in my throat. We are at a table near the log fire and the crackling is comforting, reminding me of winter evenings at Herridge Hall. I only lived there for a little over four months but I feel homesick for the house and gardens, as well as for the people.

'Ava, I'm so sorry for hurting you.'

I meet his beautiful eyes and see that he means it.

'Thank you. But I'm OK.' I shrug as if it all means nothing, and I fall in love every day.

'I'm not.' He frowns and I feel the strength I pulled together in the car ebb away like sand with the tide.

'Aren't you?' My voice sounds weak and wobbly.

Edward shakes his head. 'I feel terrible. The house is so empty without you there. Joe is lost. I... I was a fool to let you leave.'

'Edward, you can't buy everyone, you know!' I slam my hand on the table and my wine slops over the edge of the glass.

'God, no, Ava, I didn't mean it like that. I should have told you how much you mean to me. I would never have tried to force you to stay, but I could have tried to persuade you. But when we... made love... I got scared.'

'Do you think I didn't? It's been a long time since I slept with anyone... and with you... I gave myself completely.'

'I did too. At the time and then afterwards, it hit me how much I had to lose. Having been there once, I couldn't face going through it a second time and... irony of all ironies... here I am suffering because I can't stop thinking about you.'

A tear trickles down my cheek so I wipe it away. 'Tell me then, Edward. Explain to me why you were afraid. Let me understand you better. I don't want to spend the rest of my life not knowing why you let me go. Why you slept with me then pulled away as if I meant nothing to you.'

He takes a slug of wine. 'Lucille and I were young when we got together. I fell in love quickly but I didn't get to know her properly. I only knew a version of her. She was a glamorous model with her own money and career, and she seemed to genuinely like me. It's tough when you have money because people gravitate towards you because of it and over the years I've spent a lot of time dealing with people who don't want to know the real me.'

'Women you mean?'

'Women looking for a rich husband or a quick fix to their problems.'

'And you thought that was me too?'

'No. Not you. You wanted to work and then when I proposed to you I could see that you were struggling. For you, it wasn't about the money at all. But that was even harder to deal with because you seemed to genuinely care. I tried to fool myself into thinking it was just the money, the house and the land but when you left, there was no denying that this wasn't about any of that for you. You're a caring person and you wear your heart on your sleeve.'

'My mum has always said that with me what you see is what you get.'

'For me though... that was hard to understand. I never meet people who're that straightforward. It made me afraid to believe in you and in us in case it wasn't real.'

Silence falls between us, stretching out like smoke carried on the breeze.

'I have fears too, Edward.'

'I know. Your mum explained some of it. She said that your father abandoned the three of you and that you became very insular. I should have asked you to tell me before. I knew you had pain in your past but I was so caught up in trying to find reasons to justify pushing you away that I missed my chance. And then, you left and I felt like I'd completely misread everything. I'm an idiot and I know I sabotaged my chance of happiness with you.'

'I did become insular because I was terrified of letting anyone in. I saw my mum go through hell, even though she tried to hide it from me, and then when I was at school, we were researching for a project and I came across an article online about a rock band. My father was the guitarist and he looked so... happy and free, like he was having the best time.

He'd left us to go and party and it made me furious. He came back though, many times, and each time I'd see Mum shrink a little bit more when he left. She kept on hoping that he'd change, kept giving him another chance and every time he threw it back in her face. Then Mum got ill and I was so caught up in caring for her and trying to pay the bills that I had no time for anything else. I don't begrudge Mum or Daniel a second of the time I've given to caring for them, but I do have to push my anger towards my father aside on a daily basis. I don't even know where he is now and I don't want to know. But yes, the way he hurt us meant that I never wanted to fall in love and give someone that much power over me. Until I met you.'

'Ava... There's more.' His eyes are shining and I want to hug him but I need to hear what else he has to say so I hold back. 'Lucille was an amazing woman but she didn't love me. I don't think she ever did. She liked the idea of me but not the fact that I worked so hard and was often at the office or away for business. She had... ways of filling her time. I knew she'd taken cocaine recreationally before we got together. I didn't know she dabbled with other things too and after we married. Never around Joe or when she was pregnant, thank fuck, but when she was out with friends. And see... there was someone else.'

'What?'

'The night she died in Spain, she was found in the car with another man. I assumed he was a friend, possibly a colleague, but when they gave me her belongings after the crash, there were explicit messages from him on her phone. And photographs. The type of photographs a man never wants to see of his wife with someone else. I'm sure she would have deleted them... not that I ever went through her phone when she was alive... but I was grieving and desperately trying to piece together her last few days. And so... I lost her in two ways that day.'

I reach out and place my hand over his. 'I'm so sorry.'

He swallows and his Adam's apple bobs. 'I've never told anyone because I don't want Joe to know. I deleted all the photographs and messages and destroyed the phone. Her lover's phone was destroyed in the crash, so I didn't need to worry about anyone seeing the same things on that.'

'I can understand why you've struggled. Your loss was double-edged.'

'It took me a while to accept it and I was furious that she'd been cheating but then, the more I thought about things, the more I could see the signs I'd ignored. It was hard to admit but I had to accept that I'd chosen to turn a blind eye to things that I should have questioned. Being hurt and betrayed like that makes you afraid to trust anyone ever again. Lucille was unhappy with me, and I wish she'd just told me so then we could have parted amicably for Joe. But I think she liked the lifestyle, as well as the security I offered, too much to walk away from it.'

He squeezes my hand. 'Unlike you. If things aren't going the way that makes you happy, you walk away and I admire that.'

'I can't be fake, Edward. There was no way I could live with you and pretend not to care about you. Leaving you and Joe behind was the hardest thing I've ever done but it was the only way I could live with myself.'

'Do you hate me now?' he asks.

'How could I hate you? I love you but I can't be what you want me to be. I'm sorry.'

'I'm not asking you to be anything other than yourself. Please come back to me. To us.'

'I can't sign a contract agreeing to a marriage of convenience, Edward.'

'I don't want you to sign anything, Ava.' His eyes are filled with myriad emotions, and I can hear the plea in his voice. 'I'm not even asking you to marry me... not unless you want to. But please, come home with me.'

Come home with me...

Words I have longed to hear for weeks. The man I love is sitting here, holding my hand and asking me to be with him.

No contract. No fake marriage. To be with him for love.

I get up and wrap my arms around him and he buries his face in me and squeezes me tight.

'I love you, Edward. Of course I'll come home with you.'

Chapter 54

EPILOGUE

Standing on the terrace, gazing out at the land, I am overwhelmed by how beautiful March is at Herridge Hall. Daffodils and tulips grow in pots and borders, bright yellows, reds, pinks and purples. The fruit trees in the orchard are heavy with blossom and the air is mild with the promise of warmer months ahead.

I laugh as Joe runs across the grass with his new friend, four-year-old rescue greyhound, Kismet. The beautiful black dog came from the local greyhound rescue sanctuary having been surrendered there by the owner after she was no longer fast enough on the race track. Kismet has been living with us for three weeks now and she and Joe are already best friends. She sleeps in his room, follows me around during the day when he is at school, then wags her long tail in wide arcs when he returns in the afternoons. She's a beautiful, gentle creature and I love seeing her with Joe.

The rescue sanctuary was also looking for someone to run their buddy system, an initiative that involves recruiting members of the public to spend time with their dogs —

walking and grooming them as well as taking them to stay in their homes for short periods of time. It's a voluntary role and I've applied to do it because I have so much and I want to give something back. Who knows, we might even decide to foster dogs ourselves. We certainly have plenty of room.

After Edward came to speak to me, I agreed to move back in with him and Joe. We spoke to Mum together and asked how she'd feel about living at the house and she smiled but I could see the reluctance in her eyes. So instead, Edward has given her one of the properties on the estate. It's a cosy two-bedroom cottage that belonged to one of the former grooms. It had been empty for a while so Edward had it renovated and now it's a lovely home. And though they've tried to keep it quiet, Mum and Jeff have been out for dinner a few times. I've seen them together, the way he makes her laugh and blush and she's still a young woman so who knows what could happen between them. Life is for living, right?

Daniel has settled in well at his new school. Edward wanted to send him to the same school as Joe, but Mum said she'd prefer him to attend the village primary school so he can make some friends there. She got an electric bike so she can take him every morning and collect him at the end of each day and the fresh air and activity is doing her good. The movement has helped with the swelling caused by the lymphoedema and while she still has some bad days with the fibromyalgia, Edward has got her in with a specialist who is investigating what can be done to help with the pain. It can't be cured but there are some experimental treatments and medications that can ease the symptoms. It's money that has helped with this and while I wish it wasn't this way, I'm glad to see her able to enjoy life more.

As for my father, somehow, he heard about the fact that

we'd moved from Brixton and he sent me an email via Cavendish Construction. He was clearly more interested in me now due to my engagement to a billionaire CEO. I still don't know how to feel about him because anger and disappointment are my default emotions where he's concerned. Ever forgiving, Mum said to meet him and hear him out but I'm wary. The last thing I want is for him to come back into our lives and hurt us all again. And so I'm not rushing into anything. I do want to let my negative feelings towards him go so I can truly move on but it will be on my terms and with Mum and Daniel's welfare in mind. If my father wants to have contact with us then it's time for him to put in the work. He has a lot to prove and a lot of making up to do.

Since my return, Edward and I have talked lots. Initially, I was against marrying him but sleeping in his arms every night made me realise that I want to be his wife and so, when he got down on one knee again and asked me to be his wife for real, I said yes. He hasn't asked me to sign anything, but for his lawyer's peace of mind, I asked for a prenup that will protect him, and importantly Joe, should I ever run off with someone else.

That is NEVER going to happen, by the way! I love this man with my heart, mind, body and soul and I'm never letting him go.

'What're you daydreaming about?' Edward wraps his arms around me from behind and nuzzles my neck making tingles run up and down my spine.

'Our wedding. Should we have it here?'

'I don't see why not.'

He didn't marry Lucille here. They got married on a beach in St Lucia and Edward paid for all their friends and family to be present. Lucille pocketed the money from the magazine that made the highest bid for exclusivity of the wedding coverage. We won't have media present at our wedding, just a local photographer who'll capture our special day for us to look back on in years to come.

'What time is the wedding planner due to get here?' I ask.

Edward looks at his watch and I see the cufflink on his left sleeve. He wears the ones I bought him for Christmas every day, Prince Charming and his Cinderella, just like us. 'She should be here soon.'

We decided to hire a wedding planner because we don't have much time if we're to marry before Edward turns thirty-five in May. That way he'll still meet the inheritance clause and get his grandpa's shares in Cavendish Construction as well as be voted in as CEO.

'What's her name again?' I turn in his arms and gaze at his handsome face.

He frowns. 'Grace Connelly? No, Grace Cosgrove. She seems very down to earth and comes highly recommended. I think you'll get on well.'

'Sounds good to me.'

Wrapping my arms around his neck, I gaze into his brown eyes.

'I love you, Edward.'

'I love you, Ava.'

My life has changed beyond recognition.

I am grateful for every day with this wonderful man.

My life is a fairy tale come true.

Who'd have thought I'd get my happy ever after when it all started with meeting the billionaire boss...

Grab your copies of the next two books in the hot new series ***In the Name of Love*** now:

Wynter Wilde

Book 2 - Grace and Jack's story in Healing the Billionaire's Heart

Book 3 - Lucas and Carla's story in Starting Over with the Billionaire

Also by Wynter Wilde

<u>Healing the Billionaire's Heart</u>

<u>In the Name of Love Book 2</u>

Jack Kendrick: These days, I guess I'm what they refer to as a sworn bachelor. Finding my teenage sweetheart in bed with my so-called best friend led me to rule out relationships. There's no way any woman is ever going to hurt me like that again. All I want to focus on is building my business empire and having a good time.
Grace Cosgrove: As wedding planner, you'd think I'd love weddings. I used to, until my mogul fiancé dumped me at the altar. Every wedding I plan breaks my heart a little bit more and I don't think I'll ever feel joy in my job or my non-existent romantic life again.
Jack: There's a wedding on the horizon and as best man, I have to get involved. I'm not overjoyed at the prospect but when I see the wedding planner... well... sparks fly in more

Also by Wynter Wilde

ways than one. The groom tells me I'd better leave her alone, but I find her simply irresistible.

Grace: This could be the wedding of the year, a real-life Cinderella story, and they've chosen me to plan the wedding. It's brilliant for business, but it also means I have to summon some enthusiasm. Then I meet the best man and I wish he'd stop looking at me like that because I'm struggling to focus as it is.

Will Grace heal Jack's heart, or will they go their separate ways before the wedding speeches are done?

STARTING OVER WITH THE BILLIONAIRE

In the Name of Love Book 3

Lucas Barrett: I've a head for business and a body for... well, having a good time. By day, I rule the boardroom. By night, I rule the bedroom. The women I date have no expectations of me and I have none of them. Any hint of one of them wanting more and that's the last they'll see of me.

Carla Russell: After over a decade in New York, I've returned to London. It's not what I wanted but sometimes life doesn't work out the way we planned. I fell in love, got married and we talked about starting a family, but tragedy struck and my world fell apart. All I'm certain about now is that I gave my heart once and I know I'll never love again.

Lucas: When I bump into a school friend's younger sister at a bar, I consider hitting on her but there's something in her eyes that warns me not to even try. Instead, I find myself offering her a place to stay until she can get back on her feet.

Carla: Staying at the luxury city apartment of my older brother's friend was not part of the plan but when I meet him at a bar, I find I'm curious. He was an obnoxious teenager and I used to hate his guts but now he's all grown up and undeniably hot. Plus, it's the coldest winter in years, I have nowhere else to go because the hotels are all full and there's a snowstorm on the way.

Will Carla find a way to start over with the billionaire or will she leave him behind as the snow begins to melt?

Printed in Great Britain
by Amazon